NAUGHTY SPANKING THREE

A collection of twenty erotic stories

Edited by Miranda Forbes

Published by Accent Press Ltd – 2009
ISBN 9781906373702

Printed and bound in the UK

Cover Design by
Red Dot Design

Contents

In Praise of Older Women	Laurel Aspen	1
Four and a Half Acre Wood	Congressio	16
Hunger	Elizabeth Cage	29
Not Plan A	Ruth Hunt	39
Sole Indiscretion	Elizabeth Coldwell	47
Merrilee Swings	Eleanor Powell	55
Imagine	Beverly Langland	63
Once More With Feeling!	Teresa Joseph	76
Him	Cyanne	89
Learning her Lesson	Chloe Devlin	95
Sprung	Deva Shore	104
The Governess	Izzy French	113
The Rose	Beth Anderson	123
No Smoking	Stephen Albrow	127
The Worm Turns	Beverly Langland	137
Sleeping Beauty	Heather Davidson	147
A Caning for the Goddess	Alexia Falkendown	155
The Psychiatrist	Heather Davidson	169
Hard Times at the Nympho-maniac Rehabilitation Facility	K.D. Grace	175
Truly Scrumptious	Mark Ramsden	188

Contents

In Praise of Older Women
by Laurel Aspen

Fortunately the train was slowing as it approached the station or what followed might not have turned out so fortuitously. There were few passengers at this early hour of the morning, just two in the front coach; one standing ready to depart, the other seated.

With no warning the carriage shuddered to an abrupt halt. Safe in his seat, Jake lurched sideways but the standing passenger was sent hurtling down the aisle. Instinctively Jake reached out and caught her, briefly aware of an altogether pleasingly yielding body enhanced by a pleasant perfume. A brief confusion of limbs ensued before the carriage became stationary, depositing the unfortunate female bottom up and head down across Jake's lap.

As he helped her up Jake looked closely at the lady for the first time. Nicely preserved, late 40s at a guess, sleek auburn hair, and a curvaceous figure with her full, firm bottom cheeks. She wore a black wool dress and matching jacket, Prada heels, small gold hoops in her ears and a similar plain band on her finger.

The woman staggered to her feet allowing Jake to conclude his impromptu assessment: an attractive face enhanced by sparse makeup which made no attempt to conceal a few character-enhancing lines around her sparkling green eyes. Catching his glance she dissolved into laughter at the very English slapstick comedy of their situation. 'Oh goodness,' she exclaimed, 'I was scared witless for a moment there, what an undignified posture to end up in'. 'But not without its funny side,' agreed Jake, 'Whoops,' he added as the train lurched forward, 'we're moving again.'

Moments later the pair were standing on a station platform

Jake took the initiative: 'Coffee?' he suggested, raising his eyes to indicate the street above. 'I think I've had enough of the Underground. Jake Sinclair by the way,' he added by way of a belated introduction, proffering his hand.

Her warm palm grasped it enthusiastically. 'Coffee sounds great,' she said, 'I'm going to be hopelessly late for the office but after all that I need the caffeine. Annette Robinson, very pleased to make your acquaintance. Mind you,' she smiled wickedly, 'I'm not sure of the precise etiquette of an introduction to a young man after you've been across his knee.'

A small bell rang at the back of Jake's brain, the gestation of the merest flicker of the possibility of an idea, 'After you,' he said politely and thoroughly enjoyed watching her shapely behind sashay elegantly up the stairs in front of him. As compensation for their subterranean fright they opted for a seat in the bright spring sunshine. Annette delicately sipped her coffee and sat back with a contented sigh, crossing her legs in the process and causing her skirt to ride up just far enough to reveal an elegantly sculptured pair of pins.

'Thanks, Jake,' she said graciously, 'for saving me and being jolly chivalrous.'

'Not at all,' he replied, 'to be honest, I rather enjoyed it.'

'Would the experience have been so pleasurable with a 16-stone-rugby player in your lap?' enquired Annette archly.

'Fair point,' conceded Jake, 'I have to admit being in close proximity to a pretty women certainly enhanced the moment.'

'Please,' Annette raised her hand, 'I wasn't fishing for flattering comments. Not they aren't welcome, nonetheless,' she added quickly. 'Now I'm over the shock I can't help finding the whole incident amusing, and it's not as if that was the first time I've found myself across a man's knee.'

'That's a bold admission,' Jake responded guardedly, careful not to betray his excitement as this intimate, revelatory bombshell was tossed casually into their conversation.

'Well, it's easier to talk to strangers,' said Annette, 'or so popular wisdom has it.' She fell silent, her expression melancholy and wistful.

'You didn't make that remark by accident,' Jake ventured after a decent interval. 'I'm listening if you want to unburden.'

'Our narrow escape back there on the train reminded me of how much fun I once had,' said Annette. 'My husband used to be quite the dominant, I never knew how far he'd go. Spanked, or worse, until his arm tired or he saw fit to halt, then rogered, rough and ready.'

'He's not,' Jake fumbled for diplomatic words, 'Ill or dead?'

'Bless your tact, not dead, no, a fate far worse.' She laughed sarcastically, 'I'm a sodding golf widow.'

'And you're telling me because..?' Jake enquired carefully.

'Because fate might just have presented me with an opportunity for one last sexual adventure, is it possible you'd be interested?' Abruptly Annette's confidence seemed to evaporate, 'I mean I know the age gap is pretty

3

big, I'm 50, you're what, 30 and rather gorgeous?'

'Twenty-nine,' Jake gently interrupted her, aware that the power now lay squarely with him.

'My boobs used to be higher, my waist smaller and my bum less cushioned but even if I say so myself these legs are pretty good and...'

'Annette stop!' demanded Jake 'You're the epitome of the gorgeous older woman – a literal Mrs Robinson. Of course I find you desirable, and we appear to share certain, er, erotic preferences. Vanilla's not the only flavour and I'm not a total stranger to the sensual art of spanking. I'll happily take you to task, but to be honest I'm not on for a long-term relationship.'

'No that's fine, thanks for being completely candid,' Annette's face lit up with relief and anticipation. 'I don't want to exploit you or delude myself. Don't want you around long enough to go off me. Just one exciting, not-too-brief encounter is all I ask.'

'You're on, carpe diem,' confirmed Jake. A very pregnant pause ensued.

'So, um, how shall we go about it?' Annette ventured at last.

'OK, here's a plan,' suggested Jake, thinking on his feet. 'Are you free anytime at all during the day, what was it you do?'

'Yes, and let's just say "businesswoman". Talking about work or our other lives is too boring and complicated.' Annette answered.

'Agreed, keep the mystery and stick with the shared interests,' assented Jake. 'Suffice it to say I'm, ahem, between professional engagements.'

'And a touch impecunious? I suggest a hotel room, anonymous, upmarket and overnight – and on my credit card,' concluded Annette smoothly.

'Thanks,' said Jake simply and Annette was relieved to

note that his masculinity wasn't for a moment challenged by her volunteering to pick up the tab.

'OK,' Jake went on, 'let's meet here prior to checking-in sometime next week?'

Annette consulted her diary, 'Until 3pm next Wednesday then,' she agreed, blowing a him a kiss and elegantly departing.

Exactly one week later the couple sat at the same table, beneath a lime tree on a sun-dappled London pavement.

Annette had arrived first and had certainly made an effort to dress up to the occasion. Her freshly cut auburn hair was glossy and a retro 50s-style, designer dress emphasized her waist and flattered her figure. Her nylon-sheathed legs were elegantly crossed and a peep-toed, high-heeled, sling back dangled coquettishly from one foot as she sipped a cappuccino.

Annette greeted what she'd already come to think of as her young man affectionately. Jake, firmly grasping the initiative, returned her welcome with enthusiasm, ordered an Americano and sat down. Without preamble he spoke clearly and authoritatively: 'Good afternoon Mrs Robinson. No doubt you're wondering what is about to happen to you? Kindly pay close attention: at the hotel I shall escort you to our suite where a "do not disturb" sign will remain on the door for the duration. Once inside I intend to begin by removing your knickers, spreading your legs and punishing your bare bottom, you are going to be chastised.'

Annette gasped aloud, glancing quickly around in case anyone should have overheard. She'd no need to worry; the elderly Italian waiter had retreated inside.

Annette's green eyes widened, despite her initial attempt at sang froid she blushed, squirming in her chair and clenching her thighs with delight at the prospect of bittersweet pleasures to be visited upon her.

5

'You've gone strangely quiet,' observed Jake dryly.

Annette said nothing, her body language a far more eloquent expression of emotions. Face flushing pink she lowered her eyelashes, looked down at her painted toes. Annette's pulse quickened and she struggled to suppress the competing emotions of fear and desire. Adrenalin coursed electrically through her veins, her breasts visibly heaved beneath the black dress. What had begun as a whimsical escapade, a divinely decadent suggestion of sexual impropriety and licence now seemed fraught with darker, risky possibilities.

'If you wish to opt out with no shame nor hard feelings now, but only now, is the time,' whispered Jake softly.

Enjoying the last element of control she was likely to exercise until the morrow, Annette let her young paramour wait a moment for her reply. At last she drained her coffee and favoured Jake with a red-lipsticked smile. 'Shall we take a cab or walk?' she asked innocently, rising from her chair.

The taxi trip to the hotel was a prelude to a series of voyeuristic pleasures for Jake. The suggestive sway of Annette's undulating hips as her high heels clicked across the marble-floored lobby of their hotel. The merest suggestion of stocking top as she'd decorously alighted from their conveyance. Annette's teeteringly high heels forced her to take short, careful steps, conscious of her posture, shoulders back, calves tensed; pushing out her buttocks and bosom to their best advantage.

Suddenly she felt like an 18-year-old about to spend her first full night with a lover, her knickers already damp at the prospect. Fortunately Jake was charm and concern personified.

'Drink?' he enquired as they stood on the balcony of their room looking out on high-rise London, its office blocks still groaning with toiling masses. 'There's something deliciously decadent about an afternoon assignation,' said Annette, the first sips of Italian grape lending her courage. 'That guy over there certainly looks jealous,' said Jake, nodding in the direction of a tired middle manager gazing blankly in their direction from the nearest such building only 50 feet or so away. 'Let's give him a little treat.'

Setting down his drink he stepped smartly over and turned Annette gently by the shoulders until her back faced the hapless executive. Initially distracted by a kiss on her lips, too late Annette divined Jake's ulterior motive as in one smooth movement his hands slid from her upper arms, down over her bounteous curves and, grasping the hem of her dress, raised it to her waist.

'Bloody hell,' the watching executive gawped open-mouthed, the lucky young devil over yonder was no doubt about to give that fine-looking female a bloody good seeing to.

On the balcony Annette's eyes blazed fiercely. 'You rotten sod,' she said vehemently, 'I didn't agree to an audience,' and to emphasize her point she slapped Jake across the cheek.

'Splendid,' announced Jake coolly, 'exactly what I predicted you'd do. Your striking the first blow gives me just the opportunity I was waiting for.' He pulled her firmly into the hotel room and lowered the blinds.

Immediately Annette found herself back over Jake's knee, head down, fingers and toes touching the floor and the hem of her dress once more hoisted to her waist. Ten minutes is a long time to spend staring helplessly at the carpet while one's bottom is comprehensively smacked.

The sharply stinging heat in her rear drew an increasingly animated reaction; her previously well-groomed poise deserting her. Annette yelped and moaned at each percussive impact, twisting desperately across Jake's lap. Knickers twisting tightly between the cheeks of her now blush-pink bottom, heaving breasts visible as the top fastening of her dress came undone. No longer worried about the undignified exhibition she presented, Annette sought only to assuage the almost unbearable smart in her poor punished rear.

Jake eventually took the stinging sensation in his palm as an indication that sufficient chastisement had been delivered, for the moment. Lifting Annette from his lap he savoured the sight of her agitatedly hopping from foot to high-heeled foot, frantically rubbed her glowing buttocks.

'Oooh,' she complained, 'even allowing for my being out of practice you didn't have to start off so hard!'

'I'll be the judge of that,' replied Jake firmly, 'besides,' he added with a conspiratorial grin, 'something about your expression makes me think the after-effects aren't entirely unpleasant?'

'You may just have a point there,' Annette agreed ruefully; aside from the smart a familiar feeling of arousal was beginning to suffuse her most intimate parts. 'Perhaps you'd like to come and kiss me better?' she ventured hopefully.

'All in good time,' responded Jake, manfully resisting the lure of a full, pink bottom barely contained by almost translucent ivory knickers and tapering down to trim tan stocking-sheathed thighs. 'However, I believe in putting the waiting into wanting; first we'll take a little trip out for a meal.'

'Oh Christ! How can I concentrate on food and conversation when I'm this turned on?' she groaned.

'I don't know, but I'm sure I'll enjoying watching how uncomfortably you sit in the restaurant,' said Jake nonchalantly.

Rotten devil, thought Annette, wisely keeping the insult

to herself for in reality she found the situation strangely liberating, a reversal of her usual role of being in total control. Jake's effortless direction of events freed Annette from all responsibility for what might subsequently occur, allowing her imagination to savour the wistful joys of anticipation.

Thus it was that an unsatiated, hot and bothered woman walked, rather stiffly, from the hotel on the arm of her somewhat smug-looking young beau.

Despite whispered warnings to behave Annette fidgeted restlessly on the rear seat of the black cab. 'How can I keep still,' she protested plaintively, 'my bottom's burning and I'm frustrated!'

'Behave yourself, we're in public,' Jake admonished sternly.

Annette spent the rest of the short ride in petulant silence but gradually thawed with the aid of red wine and food at the restaurant and was fully restored to her newfound coquettish self by the time dessert was served, whereupon Jake got his next surprise.

Returning from a trip to powder her nose Annette inconspicuously pressed a lacy scrap of material into his palm.

'A handkerchief?' enquired Jake, puzzled. A subsequent visual inspection was enough to quickly disabuse him and with the unmistakable scent of female arousal strong in his nostrils he hastily stuffed the knickers into his pocket and turned to interrogate the strumpet seated opposite him. Jake leaned forward and spoke quietly: 'When we get back to the hotel, Annette, I am going to smack your bare bottom very hard for this impudence.'

'I expected nothing less,' she countered, slipping a dainty, nylon-clad foot from the confines of her shoe and beneath the tablecloth stretched her leg until five scarlet-painted toes were planted firmly in his groin.

'Too late to stop now,' she said, deliberately knocking his napkin to the floor.

Instinctively Jake bent to pick it up and was rewarded with a clear view up his paramour's skirt, past tightly suspendered stocking tops to her naked, visibly damp vagina.

'Isn't it about time you took me back to the hotel and dealt with me severely?' Annette queried huskily.

'Waiter, the bill please,' called Jake.

Grasped firmly by the wrist Annette was propelled, mildly tipsy, into their hotel whereupon Jake attached the promised 'do not disturb' sign to the handle and firmly locked the door.

'The reckoning,' he announced crisply, turning to face his putative punishee, 'and you can forget all about a preliminary warm-up spanking.'

'I was rather hoping for a good seeing-too,' Annette purred in her most seductive tones.

'Well you're getting a sound dose of good old-fashioned discipline first,' Jake growled.

'Uh oh,' Annette gulped, she was for it now, the extremes of pain and pleasure, just as she'd fantasised countless times over the last week.

Calmly, deliberately, Jake placed a straight-backed upholstered chair in the window, facing towards the anonymous office block whose lonely occupant they'd so entranced earlier in the day. Jake bade her kneel and, meekly yielding to disciplinary fate, Annette acquiesced to his undeniable authority. Moving with dignified elegance she knelt, lifted her dress to her waist and held it there, making only the faintest sound through pursed lips as Jake ran an exploratory palm over her knickerless derriere. Peering over her shoulder, Annette watched, hardly daring to breath, as he produced a supple, surprisingly thick strap about 18 inches long.

'The heaviest of my tawses,' he announced, 'admirably suited to play havoc with a properly grown-up and delinquent bottom.'

'How many?' queried Annette, a good deal more panicky than she'd thought she'd be.

'Until I get bored with thrashing your really rather beautiful bare bottom,' averred Jake, as if the fact were obvious.

'Perhaps now your wanton behaviour in the restaurant seems ill-judged, to say the least? Grip the back of the chair tightly, try not to cry out too loudly and above all keep still.'

Annette did as Jake instructed, defiantly pushing out her curvaceous rear to meet the first of a succession of strokes. Jake worked steadily, pausing between each blow, taking the tip of the tawse in his left hand, carefully measuring his aim and then, WHACK, bringing the thick pliable leather flashing down with satisfyingly sharp cracks across her silky white skin.

Methodically he strapped her ripe, firm posterior, each successive stroke reducing the area of virgin skin unvisited by the tawse's fiery kiss until the blows began to overlap.

By which point Annette could maintain her composure no longer, plaintively crying out, weaving her buttocks in anguish and gripping the chair back until her knuckles turned white. All the while her perfect peach of a bottom was soundly punished; only when it glowed a uniform red from the summit of her now glowing moons to the tops of her stockings did Jake cease. Annette, oblivious to the dishevelled spectacle she now presented, leapt to her feet, hands frantically massaging her blazing rear for the second time that day, dark, curly and discernibly damp pubic hair blatantly on show. Eventually she ceased her impromptu jig to slump defeated against Jake who held her gently.

'Oh you beast,' she protested softly, eyes brimming but somehow summoning the ghost of smile, 'I won't be able to sit down for days.' To illustrate her point Annette took his hands and guided them to her smarting rump, wincing at even this gentle contact. 'Feel how hot you've made me,' she pouted in an injured tone.

'Indeed I can,' affirmed Jake, his roving palm gliding across her curves, the better to determine evidence of her body's treacherous arousal. 'Dangerously erect nipples too,' he confirmed, aware of her shivering at his touch, 'and a pussy that's positively sopping.'

'High time you gave it a good hard fucking then,' urged Annette crudely, shamelessly grinding her crotch against his questing digits.

'When I've completed your punishment,' agreed Jake.

'No, darling, please, I can't possibly endure any more,' wailed Annette.

'You'll take six, and you'll count them,' snapped Jake uncompromisingly, waving a slender riding crop in front of her. Dragging her to bedroom he pushed Annette roughly onto her hands and knees on the bed, divesting her of her skirt. Annette waited in trepidation, naked from the waist down, her inundated sex and bottom cleft clearly exposed to Jake's voyeuristic enjoyment, the wanton shamelessness of her pose only increasing her sexual excitement. Drinking in the site of her truly magnificent rear, Jake felt his cock stiffen to almost painful proportions.

'Six,' he intoned solemnly.

Annette thrust her livid and no doubt sore bum out defiantly. 'The ritual must take its course,' she replied throatily, 'go on, finish me off with a thorough thrashing.'

Jake nodded silently, cruelly flicking the leather flap at the crop's tip against Annette's inner thighs, drawing sharp exclamations of discomfort in response to each cruel kiss.

Slowly he drew the crop's shaft along the slit of her vagina, parting her already lubricated labial lips and making Annette gasp at the indelicate intrusion. Maintaining her position, she tensed her muscles and closed her eyes, the first stroke could only be seconds away.

WHACK!

'One!' Her voice rose several octaves.

Successive strokes followed rapidly, each harder than its predecessor. Desperately she struggled to call out the count.

'Two, Ooh!'

'Three. Argh!'

Jake blazed the crop across her full globes.

'Four, Christ!'

'Five, Wooo!'

'Six, yes, ooh!' Annette shrieked, bucking like a horse.

'Oh, but you're wet,' cried Jake, loosening his trousers he pushed the tip of his thick shaft inch by inch into her pouting pussy. Silently she thrust back her hips in invitation, attempting to skewer her sopping sex on his rampant rod.

'Time for you to be fucked to the hilt,' he gasped, lunging forward savagely.

'Oh yes, do it, Jake, do it!' Her voice was almost a scream.

Jake's strong hands stilled her writhing bottom, pulling Annette onto the strong shaft of his erect cock. Her body reared at his touch, Annette's moist slippery nether lips yielded, one moment his prick was poised between her pouting labia, the next he had sheathed it slowly, inexorably up her silky slot until her hot, expertly whipped bottom pressed firmly back into his belly. At which point, noisily, exuberantly, with a shudder of long pent-up pleasure, Annette came.

Patiently Jake waited for her excitement to ebb then, holding her haunches firmly, he continued to fuck her deeply from behind. 'Oh God, it's been so long,' murmured Annette, abandoning herself to wave after wave of enjoyment, glorying in the sensation of being filled and stretched to the limit by Jake's engorged member, and then promptly came again.

Carefully Jake turned her over, laying Annette gently on her back. She winced as her sore behind rubbed against the course fabric of the designer bedspread and moaned in ecstatic abandon when Jake grasped her nylon-clad knees, lifted her legs to her chest, spread her wide, and penetrated her cunt to the very core; thrusting determinedly until, within a few short minutes, he gave a cry of satisfied triumph and she came yet again.

'Congratulations on getting the job, you must be very pleased?' said the attractive young human resources staffer as she walked alongside Jake through the corridors of his new employer's impressive multi-storey office a couple of weeks later.

'Pleased and relieved,' announced Jake with feeling, 'it was a testing interview process.'

'You did very well against stiff competition,' explained Jake's corporate companion. 'The only remaining formality is to meet your new boss; the company's founder likes a few minutes with every new recruit.' She popped her head around a large oak door, 'yes, the MD's free to see you now.'

In retrospect it was hard to recall who had been the most surprised since both parties rallied quickly to cover their embarrassed astonishment. Not quite fast enough for the personnel officer and the MD's secretary not to detect a momentary tension in the air and exchange conspiratorially puzzled glances behind their backs.

'Welcome,' the good-looking middle-aged woman behind the desk rose to extend a hand of greeting, checking her impulse to call him Jake and just in time recalling the surname on the file in front of her. 'My name's Annette Robinson. I'm the CEO of the company.'

'Very pleased to meet you, Ms Robinson,' replied Jake levelly, taking full advantage of the few extra seconds available to him to collect himself. 'I'm absolutely sure I'll enjoy working here.'

Four and a Half Acre Wood
by Congressio

Lady Christina abruptly spurred her bay gelding into a gallop. A moment later, Anne followed suit. Heads flattened to their horses' necks, the girls gave chase across His Lordship's field, heading straight for Four and a Half Acre Wood.

No one knew why it was so called. It didn't appear by name on maps dated before 1731; the area was shown as extensively forested and simply marked "Hunting Forest". An estate map of 1732 showed the name "Four and a Half Acre Wood", but even allowing for vagueness of scale and draughtsmanship, it was clearly much larger than its name suggested. By 1985, however, it had reduced in size and the Ordnance Survey maps of around that time suggested it covered around five acres.

Lady Christina was His Lordship's trophy wife. Twenty-seven years younger, she had married for money and position. He had married to have a beautiful woman on his arm at banquets and for sex. A prostate problem, exacerbated by too many of the former, had diminished his appetite for the latter, much to Lady Christina's relief as she preferred younger, more virile men in her bed; and women too … especially her good friend and riding companion, Anne.

Unusually, given his public school upbringing, His Lordship had not discovered his wife's other sexual appetite, that most English of sins: a good, long, hard spanking on the bare buttocks. Had he done so, he would doubtless have obliged her. And he would undoubtedly have had her flog him in return. The English aristocracy seemed to have spent much of their schooling with their bottoms in the air … receiving either a firm caning or a stout buggering.

Lady Christina eased the reins and stood up in the stirrups, slowing her horse as they approached the wood. She slowed firstly to a canter, then to a trot and finally to a walk. Anne reined down her chestnut mare similarly.

"Why are we here?" she puffed, slightly breathless from their careening ride across the fields.

"I've found the perfect place," whispered Christina. "We'll dismount here and walk in. It's not far. Bring your whip."

These last words started a fire in Anne's stomach and immediately dampened the crotch of her riding breeches. She never wore knickers when riding.

They hitched the horses on long reins to some low branches, allowing them to graze on the sparse grass at the edge of the wood.

Christina led the way, carrying her riding crop and occasionally cracking it against the side of a riding boot. The whistle and crack stirred Anne's appetite and the crotch of her breeches became even wetter. As Christina ducked under a low-hanging branch, Anne could see a damp stain spreading in the V of her jodhpurs and knew Christina was getting as turned on as she was. She shivered with delight and anticipation.

They halted. "There we are. What do you think?"

Anne looked around the small glade. It was some thirty yards in diameter, ringed by the deciduous trees that had typically made up Four and a Half Acre Wood since the late eighteenth century. She noted oak, beech and horse chestnut and a walnut or two. The floor was carpeted with last year's leaves, slowly decaying into a rich leaf mould. Dotted here and there were the empty husks of horse chestnuts, so beloved of children for the quintessentially English game of conkers; she spotted several acorns too, turned brown by the passing year. Although it was now September, the canopy above their heads had not yet begun to take on its autumn colour but the fat tree seeds she could see hanging pendulous from the tips of many twigs would soon sprinkle the glade with their bright greenery amid the russets, oranges, yellows and reds of the falling leaves.

The sun struggled to penetrate the interwoven branches and leaf quilt above their heads, and what light made it through suffused the clearing with a green tinge. Moss covered several fallen trunks, adding to the greenness.

Ahead of her was an unusual branch. Around a foot thick it grew at right angles from the base of an oak tree, running parallel to the ground and at just the right height to be bent over for a spanking and more. She walked forward and saw just behind it another branch, similarly parallel to the ground and at the right distance and of the right thickness to be grasped while bent over the larger branch. Both branches were moss-covered, but the moss on the main branch was squashed and partly rubbed away in one place. Behind it there were two clear spots on the thinner branch, just where one would grip it when bent over the main branch. Anne turned to Lady Christina quickly to applaud her on her marvellous and fortuitous discovery, to find that she had come up close behind. They embraced and necked quietly for a while.

Anne broke away. "It seems you have visited here before, you little minx."

"Just twice. I'll tell you about it later. Both times were with men. But now it's just you and me."

"It looks so perfect. Let's try it out."

"Let's. But who's to go first?"

With that, Christina turned around, bent down and picked something up from the carpet of last year's leaves and seeds. She put both hands behind her back, juggled something between them then presented her fists palm down for Anne to choose.

"Pick the acorn to go first."

Anne didn't really mind which order they went in, but played along. She laid both hands over Christina's fists and struck a thinking pose.

"Hmm. Left or right? Right or left? I don't know … yes, yes, right, right!"

Lady Christina turned over both hands and opened them. There was an acorn in each.

"Cheat!" shouted Anne. "Now you must go first. And you've earned an extra six for cheating."

Christina leant forwards and kissed Anne, slipping her tongue inside her mouth.

"I knew you'd see it my way," she murmured, and handed her riding crop to Anne. "Your choice of weapon, madam."

Christina walked to the horizontal branch, unzipped her jodhpurs and eased them down her legs to the top of her riding boots. Like Anne, she worn no knickers. Inside the crotch was wet and beautifully pungent.

She bent forwards across the branch, rising on tiptoes to grasp the far branch, then settling herself ready for whatever was coming to her. The twin globes of her creamy bottom were perfectly presented for a hand-spanking and for what would follow.

Anne stuffed her crop down her left boot and flexed Christina's a couple of times before stuffing it alongside her own. She strode towards Christina's prostrate form and positioned herself on the left. She stroked Her Ladyship's smooth flesh. There were no traces from any previous flagellation, so she knew from past experience that it must have been at least a week since Christina had received the cane, although the marks of a hand-spanking would have disappeared more quickly. She ran her fingers lasciviously down the crack between Christina's cheeks, her fingernails brushing the puckered hole and then dipping briefly between the lips of the coral labia peeking coyly between Christina's thighs. They both shuddered from the sexual tension building between them.

"Ten each side to warm up," Anne announced. Christina's buttocks wiggled in anticipation. "There's no need to count these."

Anne drew her right arm back and delivered a stinging smack to Christina's left buttock. The next fell on the right cheek.

Anne waited. A faint pink blush began to show on each rounded target. A faint handprint on the otherwise unblemished surface.

The next four smacks were delivered to each cheek in turn in short order. Christina gasped with each of the last.

"Wow! I'm warming up nicely."

The pink blush was steadily reddening and covering the whole of Christina's bottom. No longer could individual prints be distinguished; they were merging into a single broad stain of cerise flesh.

Anne shifted her stance and her aim. Now, instead of swinging her arm slightly downwards, she swung upwards, catching Christina from below and in the crease between her bottom and her thighs.

"Ouch! Ouch!" sprang from Christina's lips as the pair of blows landed. The tops of her thighs were particularly sensitive. Anne waited until she saw them turning pink, knowing that as they did so, the accompanying sting was spreading upwards and downwards too.

Five more smacks then landed in quick succession,

turning the underside of Christina's bottom and the tops of her thighs cherry red.

"Double wow."

Anne wetly kissed each cheek in turn, laving her tongue over the entire surface and dipping into the crack between them. Christina wriggled and sighed.

"Well, now! What have we here?"

The deep male voice was unexpected and unnerving. Engrossed in themselves, neither Anne nor Christina had heard any approach. They had thought themselves alone and unlikely to be discovered.

Anne spun around, but Christina remained prostrate over the branch, her pert and now very red bottom evidently on show. A slow smile spread across her face. She had recognised the voice.

"Good afternoon," the intruder said, raising his cap politely above a weather-beaten face. "I'm Tom, the estate manager – Big Tom they call me. And this is my son, Tom."

Anne was flustered. Tom the estate manager seemed unperturbed by the sight of his mistress half naked and showing the after-effects of a good spanking. For his son Tom this seemed to be altogether a different affair. His eyes were sticking out and, glancing at his crotch, Anne observed that his cock was too. If Tom the estate manager was Big Tom, his son certainly wasn't Little Tom … at least not where it counted.

"Well, then," Big Tom intoned, looking at his mistress's reddened bottom. "It looks as though we arrived at the right time to lend a hand or two."

He turned to Anne. "Give me your whip and give milady's riding crop to Little Tom here."

Anne meekly pulled them from her riding boot and handed both implements over. Big Tom was a broad-shouldered man, and as he rolled up his right sleeve Anne noted solid muscle on his forearms. His biceps bulged. Little Tom copied his father, but with his left sleeve. He too was well muscled. Together, they took station either side of Lady Christina. "How many was it to be?" Big Tom asked.

"Twelve. Oh, and an extra six for cheating in the draw as to who went first."

"So, it's eighteen strokes for milady, and how many for you?"

Anne quivered. She had expected Christina to spank and thrash her, not two brawny men. She became conscious that her breeches were now very obviously stained around her crotch, and was keenly aware that both Big and Little Tom had noticed.

"Twelve."

The number came from the bent-over Lady Christina. Anne dumbly nodded in agreement. "Twelve."

"Twelve it shall be then. Now, milady, I hope you've got a firm grip of that bough. Eighteen from Tom and me will test you sorely." He chuckled at his joke.

Anne gulped. She'd expected twelve in total. Now it seemed it would be twelve from each man, twenty-four strokes all told. She rubbed her bottom, shivered and gulped again. "Oh my poor bottom," she thought.

Big Tom had Anne's riding crop and Little Tom had Christina's. Both ended in a D-shaped leather flap, but the shaft of Anne's was a square section, whilst Christina's was round. The effects of the thin whippy crops and the flat mini-paddle ends would be different. Despite her worries, Anne was intrigued to see the marks they would make on Christina's cheeks and to feel for herself the different impacts. An observer for now, she drew closer to the three others and hugged herself in anticipation.

Big and Little Tom drew back their right and left arms respectively. Big Tom let fly first, followed a split second later by Little Tom. The whistles and cracks sounded almost together and Lady Christina's bottom bounced from the impacts. Both men drew back slightly and waited.

Two thin white lines appeared, slowly turning red, each ending in a D of deep pink. There was a suggestion of a difference between the marks left by the round and square crop shafts … but not much.

"One," intoned Lady Christina.

The arms drew back again and once more let fly, Little Tom a fraction ahead of his father this time. Two more white lines appeared, just below the previous ones. As they turned red it looked to Anne like a pair of railway lines, so straight and parallel were they.

"Two."

Again the whistles and cracks were so close as to be almost undistinguishable. This time, however, the men didn't pause and delivered ten more pairs of strokes in rapid succession. Lady Christina counted each one as fast as she could. Her knuckles were white where she gripped the bough ever more tightly with each stroke. One foot briefly left the ground as each of the final lashes cracked home. At the final pair of strokes her voice broke briefly and she called "Twelve" with a small sob at the end.

She started to rise, but Big Tom put his hand on the small of her back and pushed her down again.

"That's twelve, Ma'am, but don't forget there's an extra six for cheating."

Christina sighed and settled back down, but both men stepped back as Anne came closer and inspected the slowly blistering bottom. The marks were by now highly coloured and some lashes had fallen on top of previous ones. They were all clustered around her sit-spot. Riding back would be impossible and Anne was sure Christina wouldn't be sitting comfortably for several days. She stroked the weals gently and bent her lips to each cheek, licking along each ridge. Out of the corner of one eye she noticed Little Tom adjusting the bulge in his crotch. Turning her head the other way, she saw Big Tom doing the same. A sly smile lifted the corners of her lips. This could be fun ... after the pain.

During a pause of a few minutes Christina's bottom steadily took on greater colour and from her continual shifting it was clear that the pain was sinking throughout. Nevertheless, she uttered no sound, nor did she make any attempt to rub herself.

The Toms resumed their positions and took aim again. This time the strokes fell some ten or so seconds apart, but they were not parallel to the previous twelve. Instead they landed somewhat crossways, with the leather ends smacking into the tender flesh at the top of each cheek. Lady Christina yelped with the first pairs of three, groaned at the next and screamed with the final ones. Anne noticed that her vulva peeking as it was between her reddened thighs glistened in the pallid, filtered sunlight. The scream had not been entirely of pain, but also of orgasm. Anne moved forward to caress her friend's scalded bottom, but Big and Little Toms' hands were there first, palms stroking along the lines. The fingers of both men dipped into the crevice below Christina's bottom cheeks and brushed her wet vulva, then traced up the cleft to the puckered rosebud of her anus. Christina moaned and shuddered, and her vulva glistened more as she came once again. Anne was entranced.

"Now, Miss. Your turn, I think."

Christina was helped up by Little Tom, who held her as she recovered from her twin orgasms and her whipping. Big Tom led the nervous Anne to the branch, unzipped her breeches and pulled them down to her knees.

"No knickers. I like that sort of readiness in a woman."

Trembling, Anne bent over the thick branch and gripped

the thinner one tightly.

"Relax, Miss. It'll be easier," said Tom in her left ear.

"Aye, Miss," said the other Tom in her right.

She tried to relax. The bark of the branch was rough against her pubis. She gave a little wiggle and felt a little heat begin to build inside as she was stimulated by the mossy bark.

Regardless, she was still apprehensive. Unlike Her Ladyship, there would be no warming up of Anne's bottom such as her initial hand-spanking had done. She was to receive the strokes on her unprepared flesh. Not a frequent submissive, her buttocks were soft and she felt the cane, crop and occasional birch most keenly. She gasped. The birch. She hadn't seen any, thank goodness, but had noticed some coppiced hazel at the end of the wood where they'd left the horses. Perhaps another time.

Crack! Crack!

Away with her fantasies, she hadn't heard the warning whistle of the descending crops and the blows caught her unawares.

"Ow! Ow!" she yelled. "Sorry, sorry. Wasn't ready. That's one."

The sting began to seep through, countering the growing sexual thrill she was getting from rubbing her pubis against the branch.

Another pair of lashes fell, then two and four more. The sting became a definite pain, white-hot initially, then fading to red-hot, mimicking the change of colour she knew was taking place on her bottom.

"Si ... sev ... eight," she shouted, unable to keep up with the counting, so fast had the lashes landed.

There was a pause. Strangely, the pain in her bottom seemed no worse, whilst her vagina was hotter than before. She wondered if she had reached that plateau submissives speak about.

The final four pairs of strokes landed close together, both in time and on her bottom. With the final pair she came, hard, squirting from between the lips of her vulva as she did so.

"Wow!" yelled Christina, who had recovered her balance and had been crouching down level with Anne's bottom, watching closely. Her breeches were pulled up, but only as far as the top of her thighs where they met her throbbing bottom. She was still too tender to pull them over her ridged cheeks. She washed her hand over her face and licked each of her fingers in turn. "You sprayed me! Wonderful!"

"Way to go!" shouted Little Tom, his hand stroking the lump in his groin.

"Fantastic!" thundered Big Tom, who had his hand down inside his moleskin trousers, trying to create some additional space for his penis.

Christina helped Anne upright and hugged her. "You OK?" she asked. "Silly question, really. I've never seen you come so hard before."

Anne shuddered. "I've never come like that. I've never squirted, only read about it." She rubbed her bottom, feeling each ridge with tender fingers. She counted them. Nineteen, but five ridges were higher and sorer than the others. They must be where a second lash had landed right on top of a previous one.

"Are you ready for the finale?" asked Christina.

"What finale?"

"Shagging both Toms together."

"What? One each?"

"No. Both together. For you, my darling. My treat. You see, I've had them before!"

Anne turned back towards the branch. Slightly further along from the spanking place, both Toms were sitting facing each other. They were naked from the waist down, their penises pointing skywards a few inches apart.

"Hop up here, Miss. There's a rock either side for your feet."

It was a perfect place, Anne thought. One branch offering opportunities for spanking and sex.

"Which way round?" asked Christina.

Anne looked closely at both men's penises. Big Tom's was around seven inches, thick and knobbled with veins. Little Tom's was longer, but slimmer and circumcised.

"I'll face Big Tom," announced Anne, fearing to have his fat penis in her anus. Little Tom's would be enough.

Christina boosted Anne up between the two men, spat on her fingers and applied them to Anne's anus, then licked Little Tom's penis. Anne found that the rocks Tom had mentioned were of a size and shape and handily placed for her to put a foot securely on each so as to stand with her crotch about two inches above Little Tom's long penis.

She bent her knees and lowered herself onto the pair of cocks. Little Tom spread her bottom cheeks, his hands reigniting the fires of her caning. He pushed into her first, slowly and gently. Big Tom entered her easily; she was so wet with her previous spend and other juices.

Lady Christina began to clap slowly and Anne rose and fell in time with the clapping. As her bottom slapped onto Little Tom's thighs she felt again the sting of the riding crops and this spurred her towards a second orgasm. Christina clapped faster and faster. Anne rose and fell faster and faster. It didn't take long. As she came, she felt first Little Tom and then his father explode inside her, drenching her both front and back and extinguishing her inner fires with a deluge of cum.

After a rest of some thirty minutes, the men helped the ladies manoeuvre their riding breeches over their bottoms. The tight fabric smoothed out most of the welts, but several of the double ridges were clearly noticeable from behind.

"A variation on VPL," commented Little Tom, earning him a playful cuff from his father.

The girls walked the horses back to the manor house. Neither could face riding. Both their bottoms were too sore and Anne was additionally sore from her double penetration. But, she reflected, it was a nice sort of sore.

Before dinner that evening, they changed into more formal clothes. Both chose loose-fitting gowns and French knickers for the most comfort they could achieve. They changed together in Lady Christina's room, taking the opportunity to inspect and compare their weals in several long mirrors arranged so that every side could be seen at once. Both bottoms had turned the black red of a Chateau Palmer Grand Cru Classé, with raised welts criss-crossing like the lines at a major railway junction. They stood naked, bosom to bosom, kissing deeply whilst gently but firmly rubbing a soothing cream into each other's bottom, their fingers tracing the lines and dipping into anus and vulva as they did so. The gentle frigging took their minds off the coming agony of sitting down to dinner on the rush-seated ladder-back chairs.

In the hall, before they went in to dinner, the butler whispered discreetly, as he poured a 1998 Blanc de Chateau Prieuré-Lichine, "The Estate Manager suggested that I place an extra cushion on your chairs." There was no change in his expression as he said this. Anne looked daggers at Lady Christina. "Does everyone know?" she growled. "Don't worry," grinned Her Ladyship. "Charles has a strong right arm and a stout cock too … and he's very discreet."

Despite the extra cushion, dinner was an uncomfortable affair. Anne wriggled from time to time, partly with the ache in her bottom, but also because she was remembering the feeling of a pair of cocks inside her and fantasising too about Charles' strong right arm and stout member.

Another day, maybe … when today's scars had faded.

Hunger
by Elizabeth Cage

'Do you think it's too short?' I ask, smoothing down my slinky new red dress in front of the wardrobe mirror.

Mo wrinkles her mouth uncertainly. 'Wiggle test,' she suggests.

I begin to gyrate my hips to the sound of an imaginary dance track.

'Hmmm. It rides up just far enough to show the merest hint of a stocking top, but not to the point of indecency,' she grins approvingly. 'Ready for action?'

It's a sultry summer night and even with the car windows open, it feels hot and stuffy as Mo drives into the packed car park of our local nightclub.

'Do you think Mark will be here?' I ask nervously as Mo manoeuvres awkwardly next to a shiny green sports car, narrowly missing the wing mirror.

'Kira, for God's sake,' she sighs impatiently. 'So what if he is?'

'But I don't know how I'll feel if I see him again –'

'*You* dumped *him* three weeks ago, Kira. Get over it!'

'You're right,' I mumble miserably. 'It's just that, I really miss him.'

Mo frowns. 'Correction, hun. It isn't Mark you miss. It's sex with Mark.'

She's right, of course. Mark was insatiable, and when I was with him, so was I. We did it everywhere – on trains, in hotels, sprawled across park benches, knee tremblers in shop doorways – think of a place and we had sex there. The problem was, it wasn't just me that Mark had sex with.

'Forget about Mark,' Mo says reassuringly. 'You look great. I hope he is here. Then he'll realise what he's lost by screwing around.'

We make our entrance, strutting through the kaleidoscope of flashing, swirling lights, the thump-thump of the bass sending vibrations through our bodies. Mo gestures across the crowded dance floor. 'You think your dress is short – look at that woman over there, flashing the gash.'

But my eyes are scanning the room for Mark. I wonder what the other woman – correction, women – that he shagged, were like. Sexier than me? More adventurous? Then I notice a gorgeous-looking bloke strutting his stuff, surrounded by a gathering of appreciative females. The rhythm is pounding, pulsating, and he looks cool in a black T-shirt and tight jeans. I take in the sway of his lithe, toned body.

'What a poser,' says Mo.

'Actually, I think he looks rather good,' I reply, adding, 'you could bounce a Ping-Pong ball off that tight little bum.'

'OK, so I wouldn't kick him out of bed,' admits Mo grudgingly, although I can see she has her eyes on a tall blond-haired Adonis who is watching her from the bar.

'I think I'll get a drink,' she says distractedly. 'What do you fancy? Or is that a silly question?'

It's hard to tear my gaze away from the hunky dancer. Boy, this guy can move! Most of the blokes I've dated needed six pints before they'd venture onto the dance floor and even then they'd shuffle embarrassingly from side to side. I enjoy the display while Mo is otherwise engaged.

Eventually, Mo returns with a smug look on her face.

'Kev's just asked me out.'

'Who's Kev?'

'The guy at the bar. He's really nice. He's a personal trainer at the new fitness centre.'

'Fast work, Mo, even for you.'

She grins. 'Come on, Kira. I think it's time we got on the dance floor. I want to show Kev what's on offer.'

'You shameless tart,' I tease, noting the mischievous gleam in her eye that I know so well.

We manage to find a space on the crowded dance floor, Mo starts to move towards me and we begin our routine. She dances around me and we're back to back, brushing against each other, hips touching. Then, as the music changes, she turns to face me and she bends her knees, legs apart, swaying from her waist, her bronzed arms snaking the air. I can feel people watching our little display.

'I'm enjoying this,' she whispers, glancing in Kev's direction.

'I can see that,' I laugh.

Then the tempo changes to the mournful wailing of James Blunt and Mo mutters, 'Erection section. It's a groper.' We start to walk away but predictably, Kev comes over like a bullet out of a gun and whisks Mo back onto the dance floor. I pretend to rifle through my bag, feeling self-consciously alone. As I watch the other couples, I start to wonder what Mark is doing.

I remember the last time we had sex. We'd been out for a Sunday afternoon walk in the woods when Mark suddenly pushed me against a tree, unzipped his jeans and said, 'I want you!' With hardly a glance around to see if anyone was watching (not that it would have bothered Mark – he was quite an exhibitionist) he lifted my skirt, pushed my skimpy knickers to one side and pushed eagerly inside me.

'We can't do this here,' I'd protested feebly, but he was

31

already thrusting deeper and deeper, covering my mouth with his to drown out any further protest.

And to my surprise, I discovered the thought that we might get caught turned me on even more. As he caressed my hardened nipples through my thin blouse, he gave up trying to stifle my moans of pleasure, and I came explosively, followed closely by Mark. I remembered how I was still throbbing and tingling when we straightened our clothes and continued our stroll, as if nothing had happened. I find myself getting hot again just thinking about it.

'Penny for them?'

Suddenly I realise someone is standing beside me.

'Sorry, I was miles away.'

'Somewhere nice, I hope?' I look up to see the hot dancer and I feel my face flushing furiously.

'Sitting this one out, then?'

'Er, no one has asked me – yet,' I mumble.

'Now they have,' he replies, taking my hand in his and leading me onto the dance floor. He folds his arms around me.

'My name's Leon,' he says, his voice dark and sexy.

'Kira,' I reply.

He pulls me closer to him and I can feel my breasts brushing up against his T-shirt. I can also feel something else.

He looks deeply into my eyes, searching, as if he is waiting to see how I will react to his hardness. My heart is thumping in time with the music. I can feel his breath on my neck, his hands cradling my bum as we sway from side to side. Then he kisses me. Gently, at first, exploring. Then longer and harder, and I can feel the fire between my legs that I thought only Mark could ignite.

When the music ends, he walks me back to my table. I

decide to take the bull by the horns, so to speak.

'Would you like to come out for a drink some time?' I ask uncertainly.

'I'd love to.'

'Great. How about tonight? My place.'

'Tonight? That might be awkward.'

'Oh.' I can feel the adrenaline draining away – fast.

'It's just that I came here with my brother and he's staying at my house for the next few days. I can't really abandon him.'

'No. Of course not.' My voice is flat, the frustration palpable. Damn his brother. Then again, I did come here with Mo. Perhaps she could take his brother home. When I notice her still snogging Kev, I decide there isn't much point asking her. I wonder if I will be the one without a lift back.

'Hang on, I'll have a quick word with my brother, see what can be arranged,' says Leon, disappearing briefly in the direction of the bar. Minutes later he returns, smiling. 'It's OK. I'll drop him back at the house and then we can go on to your place.'

By the time we have shared a few more slow dances, I am desperate for a good fucking. We make our way out to the crowded car park, after I've let Mo know I've made other arrangements to get home. As I thought, she's made other arrangements too – with Kev.

'Hope you don't mind sitting in the back with Ray,' says Leon. 'The front seat is piled up with his stuff. I'm helping him move out of his old flat.'

I had been looking forward to giving Leon's cock a massage while he was driving, so by now I am feeling quite irritated with his brother. I settle myself in the back seat, trying not to show my annoyance when Leon says, 'Ah, here is Ray, at last. Ray, this is Kira.'

To my surprise, I am joined in the back by another

gorgeous-looking bloke, who seems to be a slightly younger version of Leon.

'Hello, Kira,' he says in a voice that melts my insides. 'I think we might have to squeeze in next to each other. Hope you don't mind.'

He sits much closer than is necessary and I can feel the roughness of Ray's trousers brushing against my bare thighs. As the car pulls off, he rests a hand on my knee, and when I don't push it away, he lets it travel higher and higher, until it reaches the hem of my dress. For a while, he plays with the flimsy fabric, teasing me. I am not sure how to react. I'm feeling horny as hell, and what he's doing is turning me on. But I wonder what Leon would think of his brother copping a feel of his date. It's bad manners, to say the least. Soon, Ray's fingers continue to move upwards, quickly finding the insides of my thighs, which I part to allow him easier access. I am charged with anticipation as, inevitably, his fingers find my clit, stroking it through my now damp thong. I feel my muscles tightening, wanting to suck his fingers in but knowing I have to stop myself. I try to pretend it isn't happening, although this gets increasingly harder – as does Ray, I realise, when he suddenly grabs my hand and places it firmly on the stiffening bulge in his trousers. Then I catch Leon's eye in the driving mirror and realise he can see everything. Ray looks across at his brother before taking my chin gently in his hand and then pressing his mouth against mine, his tongue finding mine, tasting, probing. Leon is smiling. Well, if he doesn't mind … I can't help wondering if they make a habit of this. But I am so turned on, I really don't care if this was a set-up.

'Why don't you both come in for coffee?' I suggest.

Luckily, my flat is on the ground floor and the front door opens straight into the kitchen, where Leon grabs me by the waist and sits me on the dining table, my dress hitched up around my waist revealing my black stockings and red suspender belt. My shiny high-heel shoes are quickly removed. The two brothers look at each other with a conspiratorial smile and I wonder what they have in mind. I don't have to wait long. Lowering their heads, they each take a suspender in their teeth, manipulating it with their tongues until it snaps open. Then, simultaneously, they roll down my stockings with their mouths. The experience is so incredibly erotic, I let my head roll back, delighting in the delicious sensations as my toes, knees and ankles are kissed and caressed lovingly. Then they are up again, a mouth pressed each side of my neck, nibbling and kissing, like a pair of sex-crazed vampires, while I gasp and groan with pleasure. I feel hands, fingers, gently parting my legs, sliding my now soaking thong down my thighs, exploring the folds of my lips, my clitoris.

'Good enough to eat,' sighs Ray, and while he covers my mouth with his, Leon grabs a banana from the fruit bowl on the kitchen worktop. Spreading my legs wide, he slowly unpeels the yellow fruit before carefully inserting it, bit by bit, into my gaping pussy. I watch, wide-eyed, as it disappears inside me and Leon kneels down, pushing his tongue in, tasting, savouring.

'Delicious,' he murmurs.

'You are such a bad girl,' adds Ray.

'Exceptionally bad,' agrees his brother. 'Corrupting nice boys like us.'

'I really think some punishment is in order,' continues Ray.

I feel a tingle down my spine and in my stomach. Fear? Excitement? Anticipation?

'What do you think, bro?' asks Leon. 'A good spanking?'

'At the very least,' replies Ray.

I tremble as his strong hands encircle my waist and he lifts me deftly off the table.

'But I think she should be naked,' says Leon, pulling my skimpy dress over my head and tossing it on the floor with my stockings and lacy thong. 'That's better.'

Before I can protest, he grabs my wrists and pins them behind my back, while Ray pushes me over the edge of the table so my shapely bum is thrust upwards – exposed and vulnerable. I wonder what I have let myself in for. Mark had never tried anything he would have called kinky with me, but I have always harboured a secret desire to be dominated and spanked. Just a little. How would the reality compare? I am about to find out.

I gasp when Ray suddenly brings his hand down on my bare flesh – much harder than I am expecting.

'Ouch, that hurts!' I exclaim, surprised

'It's supposed to, darlin',' laughs Ray. 'Otherwise it wouldn't be a very good punishment, would it?'

Before I have time to think, he brings his hand down a second time. It stings even more and I can feel the blood rising to the surface of my skin. I whimper and wriggle but Leon is holding my wrists firmly.

'No point struggling,' he grins. 'Think I'm missing out on the fun here.' He grabs a discarded stocking and twists it around my hands and arms, binding them together. 'Keep still, or it will tighten,' he warns. 'Time to share the pleasure.' I try to turn my head, pleading with my eyes, but Leon just strokes my hair and smiles.

'My turn now,' he says, raising his arm.

Between them, the two brothers perform a kind of duet, raining blows in turn. The slaps continue, each one harder than the last. My skin feels like it's on fire. But I can also feel the tingling elsewhere, between my thighs, taking over my pussy. The sensations of pleasure and pain seem inexorably entwined, and I feel as if I am drowning. My head begins to spin.

'Do you think she's had enough?' wonders Leon, resting his hand.

'Maybe one more,' replies Ray. 'Each.'

The sound of hands on skin reverberates around the room. I wonder if my neighbours can hear it. Then I am lifted to my feet once more, while my tormentors gaze appreciatively at my firm breasts before each fastens a tongue to my hard nipples while fingers bury themselves inside me, banana pulp mixing with my own streaming juices. I can feel myself coming already, but I want to hang on for longer, to hold on to the intensity that is rapidly building up. My legs are shaking and they have to steady me. I am groaning, sobbing, my wrists hurting now. Leon kisses me hard on the mouth, his tongue deep inside while Ray stands behind me, cupping my breasts, pulling and pinching my nipples. While I dissolve in the sensations, I realise I am being lowered to the floor and Leon's tongue is replaced by Ray's throbbing cock. I close my mouth around it, licking, sucking and within seconds, I feel Leon's sheathed, rock-hard dick pushing inside me. I wrap my legs around his waist while he thrusts and thrusts and by now I know I can hold back no longer. I come violently, my cries muffled by Ray's rigid cock and seconds later, Leon jerks and moans. He pulls out immediately, leaving me gaping and open, and needing to be filled. Ray quickly swaps places with his brother, and I am pounded once more, while Leon gently covers my face, neck, eyes, hair with soft kisses.

'Fuck me, fuck me,' I moan.

Unlike his brother, Ray paces himself, alternating deep thrusting with slower, rhythmic movement and it isn't long before I feel my body arch and spasm. Ray judges the moment so he comes at the same time, groaning loudly. After a moment's recovery, he withdraws and I lie there, legs parted, wide open and so, so wet.

Smiling, Ray lets his fingers trail over my aching pussy with delicate strokes, each one sending a jolt of electricity through my body, leaving me shuddering and trembling. And as Ray's fingers tease my clit, Leon buries a finger deep inside me, watching with satisfaction as I squirm and writhe. I am gasping, my breathing erratic. Loud. When I am on the edge of coming again he removes it, sucks the dripping juices, pushes it back inside me and then into my mouth.

'You taste amazing,' he says.

I am dizzy with lust and sensations, and suddenly they are both licking me at once.

Two tongues circling my swollen clit, lapping, dipping into the heady mixture of my banana-infused juices, tracing an intricate pattern, dancing on me and in me.

My head spinning, I fall and drown in the intense waves that engulf me as I come quickly. Then again. And again.

'You want more?' asks Leon, his tone gently mocking, as he unties my wrists.

'Greedy girl,' says Ray. 'And we never did get that coffee.'

Not Plan A
by Ruth Hunt

I prepared the room carefully. I lit black candles. I didn't
want any of the pastel pretty floating kind, or scented
monstrosities sporting bits of fruit. They had to be black so
they could gutter and spit dangerously in the gentlest of
breezes. I burned incense. Not sweet spring perfumes or
clinging spices but patchouli for the rich, hard earth. If I'd
wanted to bring elemental witchcraft to bear on the scene I
should have made use of air and water somehow. But I
didn't and anyway, I'm not really a witch. I'm just
expecting someone.

They are guests, by the way. Just so you know. I very
seldom entertain men with their disciplinary fantasies for
money. Only those who get an additional frisson from
some 'sordid' transaction are indulged with currency. And
there is never sex. I may accept gifts occasionally but the
satisfied glow in their cheeks, the tails between their legs
hard against their bellies as they leave is all the reward I
crave. It's quite noble of me really. Actually, I don't need
the money. I work as an accounts manager for a high-
profile advertising company and I'm ludicrously well paid.
My job gives me another opportunity to impress frightened
underlings with my authority. My reputation precedes me
and none of the underlings get to blossom into cliques of
male subversion or backbiting bitches. It's a cat-eat-dog
world out there. I see my hobby (let's call it that) as just

another extension of my personality, into something more sensual and exciting than office politics.

I dressed carefully, as always. I enjoy the attention to detail, the pleasure of my own discipline, so to speak. I wore black silk panties, brief enough for titillation yet modest enough to avoid revealing accidents. A black satin over-bust corset was laced as tight as I could take it. I have a small frame and I enjoy the suffocating perversity of making my waist as tiny as possible, forcing my breasts into deliciously creamy over-spill. With great caution, I put on sheer black stockings, the denier so fine a hard look could ladder them. Lastly the shoes. Most important. I must confess to having a slight shoe fetish. In fact I have 162 pairs of shoes. Probably more than I could sensibly wear in a lifetime. Probably. You never know. Can one ever have too many pairs of shoes? A question I usually answer with a positive negative when faced with the new season's creations from Manolo Blahnik or Gucci; I'm even sadly saucer-eyed in Top Shop. For this encounter I chose towering four-inch patent black stilettos. Not a very original look, I'll admit, but they are conservative, yet stylish, and they give me height and power. Mind you, even with four extra inches, I am still only 5'6" and it gives me an enormous sense of well-being to see the men I encounter looking down on me, and still being abject.

I sipped a glass of wine while I distributed a selection of implements on glass-topped tables around the room. My lounge began to look like an up-market installation by some slack-jawed Modern Britain titled "Pervert". A paddle, a tawse, both leather; the tawse reinforced by wicked stainless steel studs. Two different types of cane – a lithe dragon bamboo with a smooth mahogany handle and a thick Kooboo reformatory cane for the less robust among the happy crowd of floor-touching thrill seekers. Not that many of them can actually touch the floor. Very few of them are fit and under forty. I lined up others, crops, straps and my personal favourite: a four-foot Edwardian schooling whip of plaited leather, given a seal of pride by its long dead maker with a gold and ivory top. The core is whalebone and it flexes like a fishing rod. The sound it makes as it slices through the air is as exquisite as the cry that follows. Pardon me, but it's a real connoisseur's piece. And like any indulgent connoisseur, I appreciate my own handiwork. Start with a nice gentle warm-up. Those especially favoured might get a good, sound spanking over my knee while I tell them how their numerous misdemeanours have earned it. I can be Madam, Miss, Mummy or Mistress and I am unflinchingly strict. After all, they've all been naughty boys at some time and they can't hide anything from me. Nor would they seek to, if they know what's good for them. After they're nice and radiant, I take a little time with the instrument, or several of my choice. Watching the blush turn to red and then crimson, stroking, whispering, admonishing, feeling the heat and breathing in the unique and luscious perfume of well-tanned hide. Watching the vivid red lines that mark the bitter path of my cane. Hearing the moans and yelps and cries, the hard breathing and the occasional exciting sob. Holding hair tightly, turning their flushed faces to mine, telling them, "You, sir, yes you, sir. Say you're sorry. You won't do that again, will you?", all the while knowing, despite the mumbled contrition, that they absolutely, positively will.

The man of the moment had arrived. His name was John. He was tall with untidy straw-blond hair and cut a dash as the kind of ugly handsome that can get away with murder. He had an astonishingly sweet smile. I poured him a drink and we made small talk while I showed him the dark, scented ambience of my room. He walked around, looking at the equipment, reaching out and briefly touching a cane or a paddle, casting his eyes over the carefully cultivated sophistication of my leather sofas and their fur cushions and the otherwise blameless ephemera of pictures and ornaments. He turned to me as I remained standing by the door. His gaze swept over me like a searchlight.

"You look like a slut," he said finally.

I stared at him, rooted to the spot. I could feel the swoop in the pit of my stomach as his dark eyes bore into me.

"You're dressed like a tart," he added, as if the statement needed further elucidation.

Outrage rose up inside me like bile. I felt myself start to colour. Obviously I don't normally have this problem with my guests, even though submissive men are often far from compliant. They can come with a long list of rigidly cultivated and often unrealistic fantasies and proscriptions that require shaking loose to be rewarding. I like to have playful and good-natured relationships, despite my firm hand. This was clearly not Plan A. I felt my scalp begin to prickle. There was nowhere to run to, especially not half naked in four-inch heels. Perhaps a little unwisely, I opened my mouth to tell him precisely what I thought of that.

"Don't you dare," he warned. "Don't you say a word."

He looked dangerous as he came close to me and I could smell his cologne in a rich mixture with his own personal scents. Man. Excited. I stayed very still with my heart beating like a hammer in my chest as he raised a large hand and caressingly encircled my throat. An involuntary frisson went through me.

"Are you going to behave?" he asked quietly, his face only inches from mine. I swallowed as I felt his other hand on my waist. I tried to look defiant.

"Well?"

A small amount of time passed. Which part of valour is discretion? The better part, that's right. I couldn't hold his gaze any longer. It was a hard look of nothing more than patient enquiry. It would go on forever. I dropped my eyes.

"Yes," I mumbled.

"Yes what?" he demanded instantly. I knew. I knew only too well. Humiliation engulfed me. My mouth was dry. I swallowed. I hesitated.

"I can't hear you," he said, leaning so close I could feel his breath on my face.

"Yes, sir," I said quietly.

"That's better," he said, his fingers still tracing spider webs on my neck. His whole body overwhelmed me. Frightening, solid, warm, hard, soft …

"I can't believe you," he said, without rancour. He dropped his hands suddenly and pulled me by the wrists to one of my sofas. He was much bigger and heavier than me and with a surprised yelp, I found myself upended, sprawling across his lap, my head momentarily buried in one of my furry cushions. I struggled to right myself, noticing one of the black candles spitting wickedly on the shelf above me. So much for witchcraft. It was no good. He'd locked one of my legs underneath his, like any good professional, and I couldn't raise myself high enough to turn.

"Please!" I cried, rather belatedly.

"Please, *sir*!" he corrected, forcing my shoulders down with one hand and pulling my knickers down with the other. "And I didn't say you could speak. Bad girls don't get to speak. Especially not ones dressed like tarts!"

I could feel him caressing my bare backside with gentle deliberation, like an artist examining a piece of sculpture for imperfections. I panted and wriggled. He held me firmer while his fingers completed their exploration. This was a trespass that should not be borne but I felt a terrible anticipation rush through me, a flood that tensed every muscle. He waited just a second longer than my

43

expectation so the first smack across my bare cheeks managed to catch me by surprise. It was a hard stinging slap that knocked the breath out of me and rocked me forward. I felt his fingers tangle into my hair and hold on, making a casual mess of the deliberate attention I had spent on it. Another smack. Then another, waiting just long enough to give each impact its full sensational spread. He kept it up until my ears were ringing with it and a voice I barely recognised as my own had begun to cry out as the heat built up with each hard stroke.

I made ineffectual attempts to cover my increasingly abused arse but this only resulted in my arm being jammed up my back, pushing my face even further into the suffocating welcome of my designer upholstery. To add to the torture he began to rake his nails across my scalded skin. I made an idiotic mental note to check people's nails in future.

"Are you going to promise me you will dress decently?" he hissed, without letting up. "Or are there other measures I should take? Are you even listening?"

"Yes sir, yes sir," I stumbled over the words and my voice began to crack.

"Or are you going to go on behaving like a slut?"

"No, sir!" I almost wailed. My legs had begun to shake.

Abruptly he stopped, catapulting my senses into a different kind of shock. I could hear my own breathing – fast and unsteady. I could hear his – controlled, even.

"Let's see, shall we?" he said. "I can smell you, bad girl." So could I. Unmistakable. Sex. I felt mortified. He gently caressed my hot cheeks with the tips of his fingers and then plunged them between my legs, fingering me. I was soaking wet and began to moan a little, opening my legs wider, as he continued his exploration. My head was buzzing and I could feel myself becoming lost. A familiar ache began. I heard him chuckle softly.

"Not what I'd call modest, are you?" he said. "I think we need to teach you a lesson you'll actually learn."

He pulled me to my feet, a teetering mess in my lovely shoes, my hair tumbling. I was having difficulty focusing. Part of me, the outraged demon dominatrix, hands in leather gloves, whips and chains and chastity, considered assaulting John with the stilettos. But she was diminishing into impotence before the better part of me, a contrite child, love seeking and eager to please. He bent me over, pulling my knickers further down. I could almost hear my beautiful stockings laddering.

Even though I couldn't see, I could tell from the sound it made cutting through the air that he'd picked the dragon bamboo from my gallery of *objets vertu*. I braced myself against the sofa. The candles flickered with the breath of it. These were only impressions as the first stroke landed with such scalding accuracy that everything but pain was driven from me. My whole body shuddered. He was using a full swing. Dimly, I was aware he was speaking.

"Six. Count them. Say 'I'm sorry for being a slut, sir'."

There was no getting out alive so I tried. But the force of each stinging stroke kept driving the right words from my head. I was conscious only of the world in a boiling torrent being striped across my arse. And of my body's shameful arousal. Cruelly, he added another stroke for each fumble, for each hesitation. I was torn between paradise and the inferno. I wasn't even aware of it when I began to cry.

Finally it was over. I ended the count at eleven. I think. I could barely stand as he pulled me upright and held on, stroking my dishevelled hair, kissing my tears away as I desperately rubbed the tingling welts on my cheeks. He cradled me gently, massively, and I curled up in comfort, hardly aware. He was speaking softly, with more kisses and soothing words, and I let him undress me.

He took his pleasure of me on the plush, soft leather. I was still in wonderland with stars for eyes. Feeling the heat, feeling him push deep inside me. Hearing him sigh as he held my hips, his fingers curling round my buttocks into raw, hot tenderness. And safe in his control, I came with a frightening intensity that he relished. We held each other in cathartic abandon until the world slowed down and came back into focus. I watched the candles flicker again and smelled patchouli and passion.

"Hi, honey, I'm home!" John looked at me and smiled his crushingly sweet smile. I pouted, shifting my weight awkwardly on the blossoming bruises.

"Hard day at the office, darling?" I said and returned his smile.

"Oh, so-so." He ruffled my hair into further tangled hilarity. "Now where's my dinner?"

Let's be honest. Everyone has character aberrations. I'm just lucky I married mine. It's good. It makes me whole. I thumped him playfully.

"Ow!" he said and looked hurt.

Sole Indiscretion
by Elizabeth Coldwell

"I hate it when beautiful women wear ugly shoes," the Professor says.

I pause in the act of setting down his coffee cup, realising that he is staring at my feet.

"Flip-flops," he continues, "are an abomination. Yes, I know they have their place, but that's on the beach, or at the swimming pool – never, never in the street or at the office. Not only do they encourage such a lazy style of walking, they offer no support to the arch of the foot and they cause the toes to claw. You're setting yourself up for all kinds of possible problems, you know, particularly as you have such high, delicate arches. Shin splints, tendonitis. I could show you diagrams ..."

I want to tell him that these aren't *just* flip-flops. They're a cut above the average cheap plastic beach shoe, with their scattering of multi-coloured jewels across the top, and until this moment I thought they were quite pretty. But he doesn't give me a chance to explain any of that. Neither does he pull open one of the hefty medical textbooks which litter his desk to show me graphic images of ruined feet. Instead, he merely says, "In future, Louise, I would appreciate it if you wore more appropriate footwear to work."

"Of course, Professor Dobinson," I reply. It's not that much of an imposition, after all, and I was warned when I took the post that the Professor is a stickler for certain rules. I've already learned that he has to have a Danish pastry with his morning coffee, but always apple, not custard or raisin, and that no one is to interrupt him between one o'clock and half-past, because that's when he meditates. And, as bosses go, he's by no means the worst on campus, unlike Dr Chaucer in the history department, who once dangled a student out of the window of his study on the fourth floor of the arts building because the boy delivered his dissertation a fortnight late, or Miss Menzies, the senior lecturer in applied mathematics, who is, quite frankly, certifiably insane. What's more, I only have to answer to the Professor for six more weeks, while his secretary recovers from an operation, and then I can go back to my usual job in the students' union office. If I have to wear boring little court shoes to keep him happy until then, I think I can cope.

I do notice, though, that he mentioned my "delicate arches" when he was lecturing me. The girls in the office mentioned that the Professor has some kind of quirk, by which I assume they mean a specific sexual taste, but though they giggle about it, they don't seem to know what it is. Perhaps he has a foot fetish, and that's why he's so concerned about my footwear? But though I watch him very closely as I trot around fetching his coffee and the morning mail, I never notice him paying any special attention to my feet. Perhaps he has learned the art of masking his interest, particularly if it has earned him a reputation among the campus gossips. But gradually I forget all about his supposed kink, and our relationship continues on a purely professional basis. Until I spend Sunday night at Danny's.

Danny and I have been seeing each other for a couple of months. He works for a TV production company as a

48

runner, a job which is firmly at the bottom of the food chain and mostly involves him running errands and fetching coffee. Which is how we meet. We keep finding ourselves queuing in the same coffee shop – me waiting for the Professor's skinny latte and apple Danish, and Danny for an eye-wateringly complicated list of drinks, muffins and pastries for the rest of his production team, and we get chatting. I've been admiring him ever since I first noticed him, with his shaggy blond hair, dirty grin and muscular legs which are usually displayed in khaki shorts cut just below the knee. We swap numbers and he invites me for dinner in a local trattoria. By the end of the week, we're having mind-blowingly energetic sex in just about every room in his flat.

Though I stay at his place a couple of nights a week, having a flatmate who's a light sleeper and has made it clear she doesn't want to be kept awake all night by our antics, I make it a rule that I always spend Sunday nights at home. It gives me the chance to have a nice long bath, iron my work clothes ready for the week ahead and make sure my shoes are polished, just in case the Professor is taking a sneaky look at my feet when I'm not paying attention.

This particular Sunday, however, is one of those Indian summer days that sometimes grace late September with their presence, and Danny invites me for a picnic in the park near his home. He's pulled out all the stops, filling his backpack with chicken legs, rice salad, strawberries and a bottle of Prosecco, and we sit beneath the trees and feed each other. I lick my fingers clean suggestively and, almost before I know it, I'm on my back, skirt hiked up, and Danny is between my legs, mouth pressed against my pussy, licking me till I have to bite my hand so my screams don't alert any nearby dog walkers to our presence. It's a perfect afternoon, and when Danny takes me back to his flat so he can fuck me thoroughly, I lose track of time passing. Before I know it, it's close to midnight. I know I should call a cab, but Danny and his nimble tongue are surprisingly persuasive, and it does seem so much easier to stay where I am, curled up in bed with him, rather than go home and sort out a fresh outfit. After all, I always carry clean knickers and a toothbrush in case I find myself in this sort of situation. What I don't have – though it doesn't seem like much of a problem as I drift off to sleep – is anything to wear on my feet when I go into the university tomorrow morning other than my pretty jewelled sandals.

It's the first thing Professor Dobinson notices, of course, even though I don't realise it as I bustle around sorting his post and gathering a file of work which needs to be photocopied. He's quiet, apparently staring into the middle distance, but for him that isn't unusual behaviour, so I don't pay much attention to it. I'm just about to leave the room when his voice breaks the silence.

"Louise, when you first started working for me, what did I specifically request?"

At first, I can't think what he means, and then I realise he's staring down at my feet. I follow his gaze, and his lecture on unsuitable footwear floods back into my mind. "Er – you asked me not to wear flip-flops," I reply.

"And you are wearing ...?"

Sandals, I want to tell him. Lovely, feminine sandals. "Flip-flops," I say, meekly.

"Indeed," he sighs. "Such a simple request, and yet you manage to disobey me."

The word "disobey" startles me, as does the emphasis he places on it. All the time I've been working for him, I've been trying to convince myself that he's kinky for women's feet, but suddenly I'm beginning to realise that his interest may lie somewhere else entirely.

"I'm afraid I'm going to have to teach you that I make my rules for a reason, and I expect them to be adhered to."

He comes round from behind his desk. "Take those appalling things off and hand them to me."

Still a little bit taken aback by this sudden change in his behaviour, I do as he asks. He looks at the sandals with distaste, as though they might rear up and bite him, and then he turns them over and examines their soles. "This one, I think," he says, half to himself, then he settles himself down in the chair which is usually occupied by whichever student has come to him for a one-to-one discussion of their course work and turns his attention firmly back to me. "Right, Louise, I want you to bend over the desk for me." As I gape at him, he adds, "Straightaway if you please. The quicker you do as you're told, the quicker we can get this over with."

He's treating me as though I'm a naughty child who's been caught swapping notes at the back of the classroom. I'm a grown woman, and if it wasn't for the fact that he is holding my sandals, I would walk out of his office and tell the head of admin to find someone else to sort his post and fetch his bloody apple Danish. At least, I tell myself that's the reason that, instead, I position myself over his lap, face down. Otherwise, I would have to admit that there's a small part of me – well, quite a large part, actually – which believes that, yes, I have disobeyed a simple request he made when I first started working for him and, therefore, I fully deserve to take whatever punishment is coming to me. And from the way he continues to flex one of my sandals between his palms, I have a very strong suspicion as to what that punishment is going to be.

That suspicion is confirmed when, in a very matter-of-fact fashion, he lifts my skirt up so he can see the white cotton knickers which are stretched tautly across my backside. Strangely, I feel quite glad I'm wearing such ordinary underwear; if it was the skimpy, lacy pair I'd been wearing for my date with Danny yesterday, I'm sure he would have been appalled. I suspect, as with footwear, he has very decided views on such things.

Before my thoughts can wander any further, the Professor brings them sharply back to the matter in hand by tapping the sole of the sandal gently against the cheek of my bum. "A dozen, I think," he announces, and I smile to myself. How bad could a dozen slaps with a sandal really be? And then my smile fades as, with no further warning, the thin man-made sole cracks down against my backside, hard.

I yelp, and try to stand up, but the Professor's hand is firm in the small of my back, keeping me in place. "Please don't make this any harder for yourself than you have to," he sighs, and I wonder how regular a routine this is for him. How many other girls besides me has he spanked for some misdemeanour in this little cubbyhole of an office, and why has none of them ever complained? Perhaps, like me, they believed their punishment was merited.

Again I feel the sting of the despised sandal against my bum. For a man who never gives the impression of having much in the way of upper body strength, the Professor certainly has a powerful right arm. Steadily, he works his way through the first half-dozen blows, three to each cheek. I'm beginning to feel as though my flesh is on fire, prickling and burning from the force of the slaps. It might be my imagination, but I can almost swear I can feel the Professor's cock, starting to thicken and swell and press against my belly. If he is getting any kind of sexual kick from this, though, his face and demeanour are giving none of it away.

When he pauses, I begin to plead with him. "Please, you really don't need to hit me any more. I won't wear them to work again, I promise. I'm really sorry I didn't do as you asked."

"Pretty words, Louise," he replies, "but I need to know

that you truly mean them. And unfortunately for you, I've discovered over the years that there's only one way to really make a lesson hit home – if you'll excuse the pun."

As he speaks, I feel him hook his fingers into my panties and begin to slide them down. "No, please, you don't have to ..." I beg, but he is oblivious to my words as he relentlessly bares my bottom.

His hands caress my cheeks almost absent-mindedly. "You do mark beautifully, Louise," he murmurs. "It's always so delightful to see a pretty white bottom burn so red."

The sole of the sandal strokes over my bum, its smooth surface igniting little flares of pain in my already overheated flesh. I know it is nothing to what I will be feeling very soon, and I try to prepare myself as best I can.

As I grit my teeth, the Professor begins to spank me in earnest once more. Thin as my knickers are, they offered a little in the way of protection, but now I really feel the full force of each slap. Tears spring to my eyes and I kick and wriggle on the Professor's lap, desperate for my punishment to be over, but now he is taking his time, allowing me to register the impact of each slap and begin to dread the next. Finally, the twelfth blow falls. He releases his grip on me, but it is a few moments before I recover the strength to move. As I lie there, I am more aware than ever of the Professor's erection, hot and solid beneath me. I wonder whether he is about to release it from his trousers, maybe even order me to suck it, but when I look at his face, it is an impassive mask. It is as though the top and bottom halves of his body belong to two entirely separate people.

All he does is hand me my sandals as I pull my knickers back up, as discreetly as I can. "Go and have a coffee break," he tells me. "Take some time to reflect on what has just happened, and think about making good on your promise to never disobey me again."

"Yes, sir," I find myself saying, as I grab my shoulder bag. Within moments, I am standing in the corridor outside the Professor's office, wondering exactly what has just taken place between us. And then I am dashing – but not for the coffee shop, as he suggested. Instead, I head for the ladies' toilets, and lock myself in a cubicle. Again my knickers come down, and I pull the powder compact from my make-up bag so I can study the marks the Professor has made on my arse – twin red splotches on the creamy flesh that are hot to my touch. The sight is strangely gratifying, like some secret badge of honour, and my fingers stray of their own volition between my legs. Surprised by the wetness I find there, I start to rub myself. It feels good – pure pleasure after the pain of my punishment – and I find myself wondering whether the Professor has ordered me out of his office so he, too, can masturbate. It shouldn't arouse me to think of him with his cock poking out of his fly, tugging at it, but it does. With everything that's just happened, it isn't long before I'm coming, clutching on to the toilet for support as my body heaves and shudders.

As I wash my face and hands in the sink, I gaze up and catch sight of my face. My eyes are bright and glistening, and I look deliciously fulfilled. Next time I see Danny, I tell myself, I'll get him to tell me something I do which secretly annoys him – and then deliberately do it. And then I'll tell him I know a very good way of dealing with girls who don't do as they're told. I'm sure he'll enjoy finding out that there's more than one use for a flip-flop ...

Merrilee Swings
by Eleanor Powell

Merrilee was so excited. She was on tenterhooks for Pete to get home from work.

She'd been surfing on the Web and had found this fantastic site called Spanking Swingers. And, oh boy, there were actually other people out there – just like her and Pete. People who wanted to meet other couples that enjoyed playing out their fantasies.

Just the thought of the fun they were going to have made her bottom tingle and her pussy pour out juices that soaked the crotch of her knickers.

So by the time she heard Pete's key in the lock, she was dressed in her sexiest lingerie.

However, not wanting to appear too eager, she had on a black velvet wraparound skirt that covered her ankles. The blouse she chose to complete the outfit was white, high necked and long sleeved.

She knew she looked every bit the prim and proper lady that she was.

Pete came in. 'What's to eat?' he asked. 'I've ...'

'How do you fancy eating this?' she interrupted, pulling her skirt apart and revealing her black nylon see-through bikini briefs.

'Roarrrrrrrrrrr!' was Pete's response as he lunged at her, pushing her across the room until the backs of her legs were pressed against the couch. He gave her one gentle

55

push and she landed sprawling onto it, her legs wide apart.

Falling to his knees, he touched her knickered pussy, stroking it gently.

'Please tongue my clit,' she silently prayed. But instead his lips made a trail of kisses up the inside of her thighs. Starting at her inner knees he kissed her lightly, up to her pussy.

Moving aside the crotch of her knickers he kissed the thick auburn curling thatch beneath. She took a sharp intake of breath.

He did this kissing journey up each leg once again. The third time he changed to licking her, leaving a wet trail behind. As he approached her throbbing pussy, she was thrusting her eager cunt towards his mouth. But to her disappointment he withdrew his mouth and let his fingers do the walking instead.

So while his right hand fingers were very lightly moving up her inner thighs, the fingers on his left hand travelled up her belly, until they found their target. Her stiffened nipples that were by now standing out like organ stops above her black quarter-cup bra stiffened even more as he rolled her nipples between his thumb and forefinger. Placing his mouth over her right tit, he sucked the nipple into his mouth, pulling on it gently until it became elongated. He then moved his mouth over to give her left tit some attention. But it was when he attempted to get both nipples into his mouth at the same time that Merrilee took action.

She loved his teasing, but when it went on for too long she decided that enough was enough. So she pulled her tits out of his mouth. Pushed him away so that he lost his balance and fell backwards. Laughing, she stood up, adjusting her skirt and said, 'Thought you were hungry' as she moved towards the kitchen.

Pete caught up with her at the kitchen door. 'You know

what happens to little girls who tease?' At six foot two he towered over her. Merrilee felt the usual flutter in her tummy. He was so masterful.

Opening her green eyes wide, she asked, 'How can you say that about me?'

'Don't you come all innocent with me, little miss,' he answered. 'It's now comeuppance time.'

'I don't know what you mean,' she sniffed loudly, putting her pretty snub-nose in the air.

By now they were both in the kitchen. His left arm encircling her slim waist Pete manoeuvred her across the kitchen until he was sitting on a high kitchen stool with her draped over his knee. Both his feet were placed firmly on the ground. Merrilee being only five foot tall found her legs were dangling. This gave her a feeling of helplessness – which she loved. With nimble fingers he pulled on the Velcro at the waist of her skirt – it fell off her in a heap onto the kitchen floor.

Her black lacy see-through briefs gave her no protection from his strong right arm, as he beat out a rapid tattoo on her quivering bottom cheeks, turning them from a delicate pink to a deep shade of red.

'I thought you'd have had enough last night. 'Cos if I remember rightly, you had some difficulty sitting down.'

'I don't know why you keep on spanking me, you know how much I hate it.'

He stopped spanking her.

'I might just believe that,' he said, 'if you weren't such a cheeky little brat all the time.'

'Not,' she said sulkily.

'OK, Smarty Pants, shall I stop spanking you then?'

'Piss off.'

'Swearing at me, young lady, only goes to prove that you need regular spankings.'

'You're all gob and no action.'

'I think you know better than that, Merrilee, don't you?'

Raising his right arm he rained some more spanks down on her upturned bottom, reddening it even more.

'Yeowww! That bloody hurts.'

'Watch that mouth, missy, a spanking is meant to hurt.'

He hooked his fingers into the waistband of her knickers and pulled them down to around her ankles. He then went on hand spanking her.

She was squealing so loudly that the sound of the doorbell ringing made them both jump.

'Shhh! Let's ignore it,' she suggested.

''Fraid we can't,' he said. 'I didn't get a chance to tell you when I came in, but I invited Bob and Sue round for the evening.'

'Ye gods, look at the state I'm in,' she said.

'Go and ge–'

'Hiya, the door was on the latch.' Bob and Sue had walked in.

'Oops, oh dear! Looks like bad timing,' said Bob. 'Maybe we'd better go again.'

Merrilee clambered off Pete's knee. She scooped up her discarded skirt, trying desperately to replace it, but in her panic she tried to put it on upside down; then she almost lost her balance when her knickers that were still round her ankles got in a twist and became tangled with her skirt.

'Shit!' she muttered. She rudely pushed past Bob and Sue and dived behind the couch in the lounge.

'Hey, Merrilee,' Sue said. 'Wouldn't you be able to walk better if your knickers weren't round your ankles?'

Merrilee laughed, 'Whoops, seems like you've caught me with my pants down.' She kicked off the offending pants and came out from behind the couch, completely naked from the waist down.

To hide her embarrassment she sat down hurriedly. 'Ouch!' she squealed as her sore bottom made contact with the soft couch cushion.

'Bet you didn't know how cruel Pete is to me?' she went on.

'And there was me thinking I was the only ill-treated wife round here,' said Sue.

'Sue,' said Bob warningly. 'I'll deal with you later.'

Merrilee and Pete looked at each other and burst out laughing.

Sue and Bob also started laughing.

'To think we've known each other all this time and didn't realise,' said Pete.

'Do you need some TLC, Merrilee?' asked Bob, sitting down next to her.

'I sure could do with some,' agreed Merrilee, lifting her bottom and rubbing it. 'Why, are you offering Bob?' she asked with a cheeky grin.

'You bet, if Pete and Sue don't mind.'

But Pete and Sue were already eyeing each other up.

'How about you, Sue, do you need some TLC too?' Pete asked her.

'Oh, I've been a good girl, so not been spanked for a week. Would you like to see my lily white bottom, Pete?'

'Yes please,' he said eagerly.

Leaning forward, she flipped up her skirt at the back to reveal a pair of red backless briefs.

'Wow! I'd love to make your bottom as red as your knickers,' he said.

'Well, what's stopping you?' she asked.

Taking hold of her wrist, he led her across the room – pulling out a straight-backed dining chair and sitting on it, he pulled Sue over his knee.

Meanwhile, Bob and Merrilee were also getting to know each other better.

'Stand up, Merrilee,' Bob ordered. 'Let's see your bottom.'

'Take a good look,' she said, standing up.

Bob examined her hot red quivering bottom, rubbing his hands over the shiny red globes. Then he gave his opinion.

'I don't believe that Pete has spanked you. I think I should give you a sore bottom before you need TLC.'

'It takes a man not a mouse,' said Merrilee giggling.

'I'm not a mouse,' said Bob, 'although Sue has called me a rat a few times.'

'Rob the Rat, Rob the Rat,' chanted Merrilee.

'You, young lady, deserve a sound spanking,' said Bob, pulling her over his knee. 'Wow! What a spankable bum you have.' He ran his hands over the firm hot and flushed bottom lying there over his knee.

Merrilee shivered in anticipation.

Raising his right arm he brought his hand down on her right bottom cheek; it wobbled erotically; that was swiftly followed by a slap to her left cheek.

'That hurts, you lousy rotten sod,' said Merrilee, wriggling her even more reddening bottom.

'And with a mouth like that you deserve it,' Bob said.

As Merrilee bucked over Bob's knee, she knew she was getting very aroused. Her nipples were so hard they were straining to get out of her bra, while between her legs her clit was throbbing, and knowing that her juices were soaking his trousers turned her on even more.

'What's that sticking into my side?' she asked innocently.

'You'll find out very soon,' said Bob, hoarsely. His breathing was becoming ragged. 'Maybe it's time now for that TLC I promised you.'

He stopped spanking her, letting the hands that only a moment ago had been causing her to wriggle about over his knee as she tried to escape the stinging blows now stroke her burning cheeks, making her squirm about as she became even more aroused.

Bob was squeezing her cheeks, tracing his finger around the shape of her bottom. He parted her cheeks. Slipping his finger into her very wet pulsing slit, he gently flicked her engorged clit. Removing his digit from her steaming pussy, he trailed his wet finger along the crack between her bottom cheeks, stroking her puckered hole with a gentle circular movement.

Merrilee was moaning, longing for him to slip his finger into her hole. But retracing the path his fingers had taken, he again let his wandering finger enter her sopping wet pussy. He gently opened up her vaginal lips with his thumb and forefinger of his left hand – the forefinger of his right hand entered her love passage and started to finger fuck her. Using the muscles in her vaginal walls she gripped onto his finger, while she squirmed about over his knee. His fingers moved in and out of her, while the gyrations of her bottom soon brought her to a shuddering climax.

Bob pulled her up into a sitting position. Taking her hand he placed it over the bulge in his trousers. 'Look what you've done.'

Merrilee sucked in her breath. 'You're so hard.' She deftly pulled down his zip and took his cock out from its confines. It stood to attention – thick and purple-topped and visibly throbbing. It was now her turn to get down on her knees between his legs.

Putting her thumb and forefinger around the base of his stiff prick, she slowly moved up the shaft until she reached his purple helmet. Placing her mouth over his cock she began to lick him. Her tongue was darting in and out of her mouth. She licked around his cock – back, front and sides, up and down the shaft. Then, lifting his balls, she licked under them, while at the same time she gently squeezed his balls between her finger and thumb.

Bob was groaning as her hot little mouth travelled up from base to tip of his ever more swelling cock. Finally, reaching his purple helmet, she placed her mouth over it sucking it – elongating it – bringing the blood to the surface.

His breath was coming in short gasps. She knew he was about to come. Withdrawing her mouth from around his cock, kneeling down resting her elbows on the couch, she suggested, 'Why don't you come over my sore bottom?'

Bob didn't need telling twice; he too dropped to his knees, wanking himself. Within seconds he was spurting his white cum over her waiting bottom, cooling her sore cheeks. It trickled down her crack onto her still throbbing clit. She too came.

Merrilee and Bob sat on the couch, both spent – arms around each other.

Over at the other end of the lounge, Pete and Sue were also satiated.

Yawning loudly, Merrilee said, 'Who's for a cup of cocoa?' Three hands shot up.

'I'll help you,' offered Pete. He and Merrilee went to the kitchen, leaving their two friends alone.

Two hours later, they emerged from the kitchen, looking dishevelled but very contented. The lounge was empty. A piece of paper on the table with a note written in lipstick said, 'Thanks for a fantastic evening, hope we can do it again soon. Love Bob and Sue.'

Merrilee sighed contentedly. 'Wasn't that a wonderful coincidence, darling?'

'It sure was,' he agreed. 'I'm shattered; let's go to bed.'

'That reminds me of what I was going to tell you when you got home,' she said, turning to Pete, but his gentle snores greeted her words.

She smiled to herself, thinking of the wonderful times they were going to have once she did tell him about the 'Spanking Swingers' site.

Imagine
by Beverly Langland

Suzie had the most sensuous voice. The quality drew you in, made you feel as if she were seducing you personally. It was the reason her erotic recordings were so popular. Suzie was also beautiful to behold. Gina never tired of watching her alluring lips as the girl recited with an apparent air of complete innocence. Though at the moment Gina's eyes were firmly fixed on the inviting stretch of Suzie's thighs as the young woman drove them to their illicit assignation. Occasionally, Gina shook her head in disbelief, uncertain exactly how events had led to this point. She was trembling at the memory of what she had done, yet was now more anxious at what she intended to do next.

The cold Saturday morning had started slowly. Gina had drawn the short straw for the weekend shift so she came in especially early to switch on the heaters in the freezing studio. She was busy checking equipment when Suzie arrived – late – and headed straight for the recording booth. Gina noticed the shoes first, then the seemingly endless expanse of legs. They hovered on the periphery of her vision demanding to be noticed. Suzie had a stunning body as well as her *voice*. Gina often marvelled why the young woman hadn't exploited both on the stage or film.

Suzie, full of apologies, got straight on with the sound check – a limerick to make a sailor blush. Gina looked up from the console and smiled through the glass partition just as her artiste removed her coat. She was a little taken aback – Suzie was dressed in a tight, short dress, the neckline of which plunged to reveal deep cleavage. The dress may be fine for a Friday night on the town, but was inappropriate for work, insane for the inclement weather. The poor thing must be freezing. Gina decided the outfit was far too dressy for work, far too sexy. Besides, she felt distinctly frumpy.

Suzie noticed Gina's frown. "Too dressy?" she asked.

"No." What could Gina say? It seemed impolite to ask why Suzie wore a dress instead of her usual denim and T-shirt.

Suzie seemed to read her thoughts. "Darren made me wear it."

Darren is Suzie's gorgeous husband. Gina had met him once. She remembered clearly his dark, brooding eyes, his seductive mouth, the physique ... Suddenly, she registered what Suzie had said. *Made?* She considered the clothing again. The outfit looked like something Darren would like, what any hot-blooded male would like. Didn't mankind realise how bloody cold it was? Suzie lifted a toned leg to show Gina the ridiculous open-toed stilettos. "Like?"

The question seemed intentionally vague. Did Suzie mean the shoes, her skimpy outfit or something else ...? Gina felt a lump rise in her throat. She was not averse to ogling the young and beautiful herself. She decided Suzie meant the shoes. "I'm surprised you can walk. It's icy out there."

"Darren has trained me well."

Trained? Gina shook her head. Something felt wrong. Suzie had never struck her as the submissive type. At least, Suzie always came across as a confident young woman. Yet, the shoes, the dress ... All on Darren's say-so. "You let Darren decide what you wear?"

"Sometimes. Yesterday was Darren's birthday." Suzie fondled the front of her dress. "In a way we're still celebrating. I told him that for his birthday I'd do anything he wanted for the whole weekend."

"Anything?" Gina asked, captivated. Suzie had Gina so intrigued the sound engineer had completely forgotten the recording schedule. She watched with bated breath as Suzie climbed onto the high stool, her unsuitable dress sliding higher up her trim thighs. She looked so damn sexy perched with her legs dangling haphazardly. They were still communicating via microphone and speaker through the partition. Suzie looked directly into Gina's eyes and moved her mouth close to the microphone. "*Anything*," she repeated.

Her reply seemed almost a challenge, as if Suzie wanted Gina to react. Of course, Gina's curiosity remained aroused. What would Richard do given an opportunity like that? What did Darren do? What *happened*? Perhaps innocent-seeming Suzie wasn't so naive after all. "How did that work out?" Gina tried to keep her voice casual, but realised whatever she said would appear nosy.

Suzie didn't seem to mind. "Darren took me out. In this dress, too."

Gina's eyes were once again drawn to the high hemline of Suzie's flimsy dress, to the plunged neckline. "Somewhere quiet I imagine."

"The Carlton."

Gina was genuinely surprised. The Carlton was an expensive hotel. The restaurant in particular had an excellent reputation and consequently it was often difficult to obtain a reservation. Obviously Darren wasn't the jealous type. He probably enjoyed showing off his trophy wife. No doubt, having Suzie on his arm bolstered his manhood. Gina despised men like Darren. All would be fine until Suzie got older, put on a little weight. Gina took an immediate dislike to him. "Darren likes to show you off?"

Suzie smiled. "Actually, it's me who likes to flaunt."

Gina abruptly was drawn to the way the young woman swung her legs tantalisingly on the high stool directly across from her, each arc wider than the last. So Suzie liked to exhibit? Was she showing herself off now? Gina had to admit Suzie had a body fit for display. Gina wasn't a lesbian, but she was definitely attracted to women. She supposed she must be bisexual, though she had never actually pursued a female relationship, preferring to watch from a distance. Gina reluctantly tore her eyes from the dark promise between Suzie's thighs, aware that her cheeks were a little flushed. For a moment she thought she was in danger of revealing her best-kept secret. Feeling exposed, she hurriedly searched her console for the script.

"Last night I was in my element." Suzie's voice filled the studio.

"Really?" *Where was that bloody script?*

"Do you know the Carlton? I used the open expanse between the restaurant and the cloakroom as a makeshift catwalk. You know ..."

Gina wasn't paying much attention. She was scrambling under the console for the raft of papers infuriatingly just out of reach. Eventually, she emerged, script in hand. "Sounds as if you were enjoying yourself?"

"Oh yes! It was supposed to be an evening for Darren but he treated me as if it were *my* birthday – until I went too far, that is."

"Went too far?"

"Well, too far in Darren's eyes. After another visit to the Ladies I strut back to our table, making certain I had the attention of everyone in the restaurant. Of course, I was careful to ensure the click of my heels on the tiled floor was loud enough to draw all eyes my way. By the time I reached my seat Darren was tutting and shaking his head. I could see he was angry but I did not offer an apology for my unashamed display. Instead, I lift the hem of the dress slightly and twirl. 'You don't like?' I ask. Darren raises an eyebrow. His instructions were that I should not wear any underwear. He was adamant on that point and because of my promise I obliged. Emboldened by the champagne I raise a foot onto his chair. His eyes grow wide. It is a shameless display, designed to turn him on, to turn me on."

Obviously, Suzie liked to live dangerously. Gina was getting turned on just listening to her story. "Darren didn't like that?" she asked.

"Well, yes and no ..."

"What did he say?"

"Am I to spank you again?"

Flabbergasted, Gina fell back into her chair.

"That's exactly how everyone reacted. It seemed the whole restaurant fell silent. The elderly couple at the next table stared wide-eyed; a strangled cough issued from the table behind. I ignored them. 'As you please,' I challenged. 'You're arrogant enough to feel I am yours to do with as you wish.' I know I have pushed Darren too far. My heart races as he keeps an iron grip on my hand, all but forcefully dragging me from the restaurant. I stumble behind, struggling to remain graceful in the stiletto heels."

"Goodness!" Something inside Gina wanted to keep Suzie talking. "Go on."

Suzie peered over her shoulder even though the studio door was closed; then once again leaned closer to the microphone. She talked in a lower voice. Somehow the two had become fellow conspirators. Surreptitiously Gina pressed the record button. Whatever Suzie had to say she wanted to keep for posterity. "He took me to our room and had me lean against the bed, well, sort of half lie on it ..." She looked at Gina. "You know ..."

"Not really," Gina lied.

"Like this." Suzie stepped off the stool and bent over

the end of the script desk so her body was supported by her arms, her bottom right at the edge. "And?" Gina asked.

"He had me lift my dress." Suzie took the edge of her dress with one hand and lifted the hem a couple of inches – then stopped. Gina felt an unexplained sense of disappointment. "Only that far?" The voyeur in her expected more.

Suzie giggled. "Until my bottom was bare."

"Well, what happened next?"

"You seem awfully nosy!"

Gina was too turned on to allow Suzie to stop. Snooping or not, she *had* to know what happened. "I'm curious, that's all."

"Well, Darren had me reach back and feel myself."

Gina felt she was in heaven when Suzie actually reached back and put her hand on her backside. She recalled that Suzie wore only what Darren had requested. She just *knew* Suzie was naked beneath the dress! She had to be! "My dress was up, of course," Suzie added in case Gina didn't get the full picture. Gina could imagine. She envisioned the young woman bent over the edge of the bed, touching herself. Images of the porn she occasionally watched with Richard sprang to mind. She pictured Suzie in a starring role. "Darren watched until he decided it was time to spank me."

Gina had forgotten about the threatened spanking.

"Darren moved me to the middle of the room and had me bend over and grasp my ankles. He insisted I keep my legs straight. Would you like me to show you?"

Gina's mind was a whirl of emotion. Why was Suzie doing this? Why was she responding? Normally the erotica Gina recorded didn't reach her. Stories were often recorded in disjointed segments and by the time she had the complete item the words had lost any impact. This felt different. Suzie's tale was much more personal. Gina felt absolutely wicked. She shouldn't be listening to this at all. She certainly shouldn't be recording it. "If you like." It was difficult now to conceal her arousal.

Suzie moved to the centre of the booth and bent forward so far that not only her bottom was exposed. Gina was delighted. She had a clear view of the girl's sex. Even from her sitting position on the other side of the glass partition she could make out Suzie's arousal. The bloated labia. The slight parting of lips. The glistening wetness. Obviously Suzie enjoyed the retelling of her exploits as much as Gina loved listening. The whole situation seemed far-fetched. Gina felt as if she were back in an Amsterdam sex bar she had once visited out of curiosity. The girl on the other side of the glass performed for her benefit, yet she seemed wholly disconnected, disinterested even. Still, Gina had taken voyeuristic pleasure in the girl's brazen display, safe and anonymous behind the barrier of glass. Now, as then, Gina pressed her hand between her thighs. Why not? Suzie couldn't possibly see what she was doing beneath the console. The thrill she felt was delightful. "Then what?" she encouraged.

"Darren spanked me. I'm sure you don't want to hear the details."

Gina did! Was Suzie teasing her? "I'd like to. I mean, I don't want to spoil your story."

"Well, if you *really* want?"

Suzie made no attempt to continue. She was definitely teasing, forcing Gina to admit her interest. "Yes. Yes I do!"

"Of course, no girl likes to be spanked unless she is aroused. Darren certainly had me aroused. He had let me have my fun but I sensed that the foreplay was over. So, I spread my legs wide, clasp my ankles, follow his instructions exactly – with full knowledge that in so doing I reveal myself completely. Can you imagine how it feels to be exposed and totally at Darren's mercy? Knowing how vulnerable you are. Knowing he can do whatever he desires."

"I can imagine." Gina drew open the zip of her trousers.

"Can you really?"

"Yes," she whispered. Her trembling fingers stole inside.

"I had to fight the urge to flee."

"You didn't! I mean, you didn't?"

"No. Darren stood beside me, ran a fingernail down the ridge of my spine, making me shiver, but I didn't feel threatened. He touched my bottom, his hand steady while I trembled. Next to him the lewdness of my posture feels sublimely wicked. Of course, my exposure is part of his game. 'You've been a naughty girl Suzie,' he says, patting my bottom, 'strutting around with no panties ...' I apologise, promise to be good. 'I'm afraid your apology isn't good enough. I must punish you. You are a blatant exhibitionist!'"

Gina was beginning to see Darren's point. The whole time Suzie had been telling her story, she had made no effort to cover herself. Not that Gina had any complaints. The view from the front row was exquisite. "So Darren spanked you?"

"And how! I wait while he draws back his hand, holds for a moment – what seems an eternity – drawing my sense of trepidation. Making me wait. Making me want. Making me wet. So incredibly wet! He is in no hurry. Darren understands the power of anticipation. Can you imagine how it feels to wait like that? Knowing what is to come, but never when?"

Gina was vaguely aware that her fingers were moving of their own volition.

"The first sting of his hand brings tears to my eyes. He does not hold back and I almost lose my position. I am both shocked and delighted that he dare hurt me – this man

70

who professes to love me. Hot, sharp pain flares in my cheeks, more intense than I imagined, yet fading faster. The blood rushes to my smarting buttocks, the cheeks reddening, glowing like a beacon, drawing him to me."

Gina had no problem envisaging Suzie's bottom red and smarting. Her fingers scratched against the front of her knickers. Damn the bloody things. They may be warm but all of a sudden the material felt infuriatingly obtrusive.

"The second slap is harder still. My body jerks, my eyes fly open in surprise and I let out a strangled cry. My anguished outburst excites him and with excitement come more blows – heavier blows. The pain builds, becomes needle-like, lingers until I feel I am on fire. Not only the flesh of my bottom but deep between my legs. My pussy throbs, and then the throbbing becomes a dull, needful ache. Soon the heat grows intolerable. It starts to consume me from the inside, turns against me, an agitator for his cause. Imagine how I must have looked to him?"

Gina bit her bottom lip.

"Again he strikes! The heat flares and I open my mouth in silent cry. This time the pain remains stubborn, fades reluctantly. Tears trickle from the corners of my eyes as the ache clings. Yet, somehow I harvest it. My cunt becomes the centre of my universe. Through it I am hypersensitive to the world around me. I feel the rush of air as his hand approaches; feel steamy moisture seep down the insides of my thighs. I am leaking lava. Any moment I will erupt."

Gina too felt close to erupting. It was pointless pretending otherwise. She dropped her left hand into her lap, searched frantically for the waistband of her knickers. Her masturbating hand shot inside, sought her wetness and drew it onto her clitoris. That first touch was almost too much. Gina groaned loudly.

"Are you all right?"

"Yes! Go on!"

"Well, I bite my lip. Even though I want to scream I whimper. Perhaps not as you imagine – not like a scolded child but like a bitch in heat. The sounds I make are truly pathetic; they somehow make my punishment more demeaning. Before him I am weak. I profess my love when I should be indignant, when I should challenge his assumption that I am his to do with as he pleases, that I am a possession like the Japanese bondage prints in his study. Instead, I thank him for his diligence; thank him for keeping me on the straight and narrow."

"Then he was satisfied?" Gina hoped not. Beneath the console she frantically rubbed away, building to one of the most peculiar climaxes she had ever experienced.

"No! He pulled out his cock and stood behind me."

Gina imagined Darren towering over the exposed girl, monstrous and erect. "Did he do you from behind? Men like that. How did it feel?"

"His hips press against me. Despite my resolve I gasp as the pressure makes the pain flare. I welcome the feel of his erection, close my eyes, soak up the wicked pleasure as the hard bulge presses into the crack of my seared bottom. My pussy is swollen and bloated, my breathing ragged. I am empty. I need to be filled, need to be filled by him. Even the air is heavy with my need. Darren knows. He teases me with his erection. His fingers slide slowly over my heated skin, a nail traces a lazy trail ever downwards. He lingers at my anus, making me wonder, letting me know I am his completely. His other hand slides between my thighs, inches slowly upwards. My legs tremble as he stops barely a finger's width from the outer folds of my sex. I almost swoon with desire. Suddenly he removes his hands, backs away. I open my mouth in surprise, anger and rebellion rising. 'Please!'"

"Darren left you hanging like that?"

"I grow ever more frantic. He wants me to plead – to

beg."

"Yes, beg," Gina repeated. "Did you? Did you beg?"

"Yes! I am past caring about self-respect. Only now as the pain subsides do I feel exposed, so totally at his mercy. Thankfully, Darren relents. His hand once again slides between my thighs. I gasp as an impossibly thick finger parts my lips. His finger lingers in the moistness, anticipation causing the hairs on the back of my neck to rise. He has the dexterity of a seamstress. He works me, picking at the threads holding me together until I am in danger of unravelling."

Suzie moved at last. She turned to face the glass partition, to face Gina who considered her through glazed eyes. The young woman's face is flushed, her eyes wide with excitement. "He feigns contempt at my weakness, delves deeper. I swallow his finger effortlessly, shudder in pleasure, no longer embarrassed by my body's mutiny. I would like him to give more. Two fingers, three! Fuck me, damn it, fuck me! Instead, he teases, waits until I am close to climax, withdraws. I try to clench him to me, dangerously close to the abyss. It is no use. As ever, his timing is impeccable. I must wait. I derive a perverse pleasure from his meanness. It is the reason he can play me. I plead again, fighting back my guilt. What sort of woman am I?"

"A slut," Gina called out.

Suzie smiled. "Yes! Can you imagine the cruelty of it? Not any slut – I am *his* slut he reminds me." Suzie left the recording booth to join Gina in the control room. Gina's hand froze when she realised. Suzie leaned against the console. "He did me *back there*," she said, touching her bottom again.

Gina mulled over what Suzie had said. Suddenly it registered what the girl meant. She almost swooned at the thought. Once again her fingers started to move. She didn't care any more. Suzie was in the room right next to her – watching – yet Gina didn't care. She had to finish. Suzie had to finish! "You let him?"

"I am anything Darren wants me to be. I'll do anything he wants me to do." She stared into Gina's eyes. "Shall I continue?"

"God, yes!"

"It is difficult to suppress my elation as his hands grasp my hips, draw me to him. His erection nudges my puckered flesh – rigid, imposing and rampant. Knowing how much he wants me fuels my hunger. He slips into me without hesitation, confident of his status, certain my arousal has prepared the way. His arrogance knows no bounds. In one deft movement he claims me, leaves me in no doubt I am his. I cry out, my submission complete. Darren knows me too well. Knows when to punish, when to deny, when to give, when to keep giving ... He comes deep inside me. I squeal like an alley cat, cling to him, trying to force the cork back into the bottle. It is no use. Like a volcano I erupt until I too am spent."

Gina closed her eyes. She was in the hotel room with Darren *doing* little Suzie! Suzie screaming in pleasure! Gina was mesmerised by the picture in her mind. She was on the cusp now. Rubbing frantically on her clitoris while a woman she hardly knew revealed her sex life in graphic detail. "It was ... so ... good ..." Suzie's seductive voice was close to Gina's ear. She could feel the woman's hot breath. In that instant Gina came.

After a while Gina shook herself out of her daze. Her hand was still clasped against her sex. Suzie stared at her intently. The girl didn't say anything – she just had a faraway look on her face. All Gina could think was that beneath her flimsy dress, the delectable Suzie was naked. If she could just reach out and touch ... As if reading her mind Suzie smiled and edged the dress higher. "Good?" she finally asked, her voice a little breathy.

Gina wasn't certain if Suzie referred to the story or her orgasm. "Yes," she answered.

"Would you like to join Darren and me?"

Gina swallowed hard. She couldn't answer, her mouth was too dry. "Come on ..." Suzie stood and pulled on Gina's hand. How would she ever explain taking off from work with Suzie? Yet, she was already fumbling with her trousers and searching for her coat. Sod the schedule. The day was beyond bizarre, yet what puzzled Gina most was Suzie's motivation. She had never shown any inclination of exhibitionist behaviour before, had never hinted that she too liked girls.

At the first set of traffic lights Gina got her answer. Suzie turned to Gina and squeezed her hand reassuringly. "I can see you're wondering why I'm doing this. Well ... Darren's orders this morning," Suzie whispered as she slipped the car into gear and set off once more, "were to seduce a woman and bring her back to him."

"All this was a set-up? For Darren's benefit?"

Suzie giggled. "Can you imagine how pleased he'll be?"

Gina squirmed in her seat. "Yes, I can imagine!"

Once More With Feeling!
by Teresa Joseph

Resting her head in her hands, the director sighed as she watched the actresses run through the scene yet again. This was the scene dress rehearsal. There was only a week left to go before opening night, and the damn thing *still* wasn't working.

Six months ago, the Northumbrian Women's Theatre Group had agreed to put on a stage production of the autobiography of a local feminist activist named Yolanda Jacobs. But now, at the eleventh hour, the director was seriously thinking about calling off the whole thing.

In the first part of her book, Yolanda had written about how at school in the late 1950s, she had been a nonconformist rebel until a certain schoolmistress had caned her into submission; how this mistreatment had left her a placid doormat until the dawn of Women's Lib. So in the first scene, the actress who played the young Yolanda Jacobs was to be punished repeatedly until she relented.

In technical terms, things couldn't have been better. The lines were learnt, the sets and costumes were made and the stage management was flawless. But even now after months of rehearsals, the acting was still about as wooden as a tree and as believable as the *Sunday Sport*.

They had gone through the whole scene seven times that day, but they still hadn't made any progress and the director was on the verge of blowing her top.

In her prop glasses, tweed skirt suit and five-inch high heels and with her hair up in a bun, the tall, blonde actress who played Yolanda's schoolmistress looked to be the very essence of authority. But even dressed the way she was, the woman still swung the cane as if it were a conductor's baton.

The actress who played Yolanda too, supposedly the impassioned rebel with her skirt too short and her hair too long, made no attempt to resist her punishment.

"For God's sake!" bellowed the director as she stormed up onto the stage. "How many times do we have to do this scene?"

Grabbing the cane from the teacher's hand, she gave her a good hard whack across the backside. And yelping with pain, the blonde actress grabbed hold of her buttocks and leapt six feet into the air.

"That's the way you're supposed to act when she canes you!" shouted the director, pointing the cane at the actress who was playing Jacobs.

"And Katie!" she added, turning back to the teacher. "This is how you're supposed to behave!"

Making sure that Katie had calmed down a little, the director then gave the actress another good whack across her stinging cheeks.

"Lick my trainers clean!" she ordered, threatening Katie with another whack.

"No, Mary! Stop it!" wept the actress, rubbing her bottom yet again.

"Get down on all fours and lick my trainers!" she commanded, this time caning Katie across the back of her thighs.

"No, Mary! Stop it!"

"Now!"

And with that, Mary let rip, flailing the actress's bottom,

thighs and calves relentlessly, making her sob and squeal like a baby.

Katie tried to get away, running as fast as she could in her high heels and shouting for help from the other girls on stage. But they just stood and watched as Mary jogged after her, relentlessly caning her tender flesh.

Despite running as fast as she could, there was no way for the poor girl to escape. And the harder she tried, the harder that Mary caned her.

Having taken more than thirty strokes, each one more vicious than the last, Katie collapsed down onto her knees. Sobbing pitifully, completely broken and willing to do anything to make her stop, she leaned forward and tongued the director's shoes with all her might as the tears rolled down her cheeks.

"Do you see, ladies?" asked Mary, addressing the other actresses. "I've just captured the whole spirit of the scene in one go. My anger, Katie's initial defiance, my persistence and Katie's eventual surrender, all whilst the rest of you look on in horror, is exactly what the scene demands. I have a production meeting now, and I'll be back in three hours. When I get back, I want to see a complete run-through of the scene capturing all the emotions I've just demonstrated. Any questions?"

No one on stage made a sound. They were all still too stunned by what they had just seen.

"In that case," she concluded, tossing the cane down onto the ground in front of her, "I'll see you again at seven."

The very second that Mary had left and slammed the door behind her, the others all rushed over to help Katie up.

"Are you all right?" asked Sally, the girl who played Yolanda.

"I'm fine," she sniffed as she regained her composure and dried her eyes. "But it still stings like hell though."

Lifting her skirt up around her waist and lowering her knickers, Katie showed the other girls the true extent of her caning.

Angry red lines criss-crossed her cheeks, making her bottom look like a stick of Blackpool rock laid on its side. Her thighs and calves weren't much better, and captivated by the spectacle, every girl on the stage crowded around to show Katie sympathy and to touch her red-hot weals.

As Sally gazed at her colleague's sore legs and bottom, she couldn't help but wonder how it felt. Watching Katie being chased around the room by Mary had been absolutely terrifying, but she hadn't been able to look away.

Seeing the actress being dominated so cruelly had been the most exhilarating experience of her life. And having spent her whole career pretending to be someone else, Sally wanted to experience something real for herself.

Every rational bone in her body screamed at her not to do it, but before she could think, Sally found herself suggesting an idea to Katie.

"You know, there's no way that I'm ever going to be able to fake the reactions you showed Mary," she reasoned, trying to justify her idea to herself as much as to Katie. "But if she comes back and finds us still struggling with page one, she's going to blow her top again."

Sally paused for a moment; taking a breath to calm herself before nervously making her proposal.

"If I'm going to be able to react properly," she stuttered, almost cringing at what she was saying, "then I'm going to have to feel it for myself, for real."

The other girls on stage were all doubtful. Would it really be worth it? Katie on the other hand had no qualms whatsoever. If Sally felt that having her backside set alight was the only way she'd be able to get into character before Mary came back, that was fine with her. After all, she had already been the target of the director's venom that day, and she didn't exactly fancy a second helping.

Having pulled her knickers back up and rolled down the hem of her skirt, Katie picked up the cane and waited for Sally to get ready.

Taking a deep breath as she took down her navy blue PE knickers, Sally lifted her skirt up around her waist and touched her toes. She braced herself for impact, wondering what the hell she'd gotten herself into.

"No!" She announced triumphantly. "I am *not* going to lick your shoes!"

That was Katie's cue.

Bringing her arm back as far as she could, the teacher lay a vicious and agonising stroke full square across Sally's cheeks.

Grabbing her ankles and digging her nails into her skin, Sally literally had to bite her tongue to keep herself from crying out in pain. Mary's instruction had really shown the schoolmistress a thing or two, and now there was no way that anyone could accuse her of holding back.

Having done her duty and shown Sally what it really felt like, Katie was about to call it a day. But then without hesitation, Sally delivered her second line.

"Never! I'll never submit to you!"

Sally had requested a second helping. And so in spite of her better judgement, Katie obliged.

As the second welt formed across her firm young cheeks, Sally told herself that it was all for the good of the play and that she was simply learning the role. But deep down, the woman knew that she was having the time of her life.

Even back when Sally was auditioning for the part, she had been secretly excited by the idea of being caned in front of a live audience. And now, as the class all stood in a semi circle behind her, watching silently as her sweet little peaches were punished by this merciless piece of willow, the woman was as happy as could be.

Summoning up all of her self-control, Sally resisted the urge to lick her lips as she remembered that in just a few days, she would be caned in front of an audience of two hundred, including her friends and family. The very thought of this made her shudder with delight. Even now as she felt thirty pairs of eyes fixed on her thighs and bottom, she could hardly contain herself. And standing there wincing with pain and savouring every stroke, she couldn't help but wish that they were rehearsing in public.

As the sixth and final stroke lashed across her precious cheeks, Sally sighed, apparently with relief, but inwardly with disappointment. And standing there touching her toes with the marks on her bare bottom stinging joyfully, she tried to think of a way to prolong the rehearsal.

Just as she had started to get good, Katie had stopped, leaving Sally feeling deeply unsatisfied. She could ask Katie if she fancied another run-through, but that would probably seem too blatant.

Then, just as Sally was pulling her knickers back up, one of the other schoolgirls from the scene made a suggestion.

"Erm, maybe if you really want to know how it feels to be dominated by the schoolmistress, and Katie, if you want to know what it's like to dominate someone, then maybe you should take her over your knee and spank her bottom." The girl's face turned as red as a beetroot as she tried to explain herself, only managing to dig herself in even deeper. "Er, I read somewhere that it's really humiliating and it puts you in your place. You know, like when your auntie is really angry at you for smashing her favourite vase and …"

Blushing like a twelve-year-old and stumbling over every word, the girl then decided that it was time for her to shut up.

"Yes, good idea, Carol," praised Sally, secretly thanking her for coming up with such a good excuse to continue the scene. "What do you say, Katie? Should I fetch the chair?"

Katie hesitated for a second. But then, something inside her made her agree. And fetching the chair, the teacher sat down and beckoned Sally forward as she scornfully peered over her glasses.

The welts on her bottom and thighs made it hard for her to sit down. But like the true actress she was, Katie had turned her agonised winces into subtle sneers of contempt; allowing her pain to fuel her anger at the director for caning her. And now, as Sally shuffled hesitantly into place, Katie imagined that it was Mary who was bending over her knee and that this was her chance for revenge.

Holding back a chuckle, the actress smiled a little. This was going to be good.

Sally was also trying hard not to giggle as she slowly made her way over to Katie, pulling her knickers down around the tops of her thighs and keeping her head respectfully bowed.

As the rest of the girls all shuffled into position, struggling to get a good view, Sally stood sulkily beside her teacher with her hands behind her back, looking very hard done by.

Pointing at her lap, Katie silently ordered the girl over her knee. And then pulling the hem of Sally's skirt up around her waist and her knickers right down, she laid the first melodic stroke across her painful rump.

As the first smack was laid across her stinging welts, Sally finally began to whimper with pain.

Having never done this before, Katie suddenly found that she was enjoying herself. She'd felt sure that she would need to get her revenge on Mary by proxy, but hearing Sally whine really excited the young actress and made her want to spank her even more.

The caning had all been a bit too impersonal for her liking. But feeling a submissive little schoolgirl laid across her knee; hearing her sob quietly as she smacked her ripe round cheeks made Katie tingle with pleasure.

Staying in character, the teacher tried very hard to remain stern and surly, snapping angrily at the young girl and telling her what a dirty little trollop she was, trying very hard not to grin when Sally replied with a sheepish "Yes, Miss."

Experimenting with different spanking techniques, Katie found that she was really getting the feel for it, and that a nice, rhythmic stroke across each cheek in turn was by far the most satisfying for both of them. An occasional whack with full force across both cheeks was lovely, but it stung her hand too much for her to do it very often.

Laid across her knee with her hands resting on the edge of the chair, Sally agreed with Katie that an occasional hard whack was best.

She loved the way that after half a dozen, a dozen or maybe even two dozen strokes, she might get a real belter across her bottom. The variety and the unpredictability really made it fun. What was more, lying helplessly across her teacher's knee was making her feel more like a naughty schoolgirl than she ever could have dreamed.

Having truly developed a taste for disciplining her colleague, Katie was unwilling to stop when her hand became sore. So snapping her fingers impatiently, she ordered one of the girls to fetch her a leather paddle. And of course, the excited young woman obeyed quickly, quietly and without question.

After the firm, targeted smacks of her teacher's hand, the sensation of the heavy leather paddle being laid with full force across her bottom was a real change of pace for Sally. But after the initial shock, the young actress had to bite her lip to keep herself from crying out for more.

First a dozen, then two dozen, then three dozen strokes whacked across Sally's buttocks, turning her cheeks the most delightful shade of crimson and making her cry out with pain.

As the crowd looked on, wincing with sympathy as every stroke found its mark, the fire in Sally's rump grew more painful until eventually she could no longer control herself.

She tried to hold on, to push herself to the limit, but her bottom couldn't take any more. So breaking down in tears, the actress pleaded for Katie to stop.

"Please madam!" She squealed. "I'll lick your shoes clean! Just *please* let me go!"

That was Katie's cue to let Sally up, but the schoolmistress had no intention of stopping just yet.

Her heart was pounding, her blood was surging and the look on her face was one of sadistic glee. She had the young girl in her power, she was making her dance to her tune. The sound of the paddle against her sweet, tender flesh was music to her ears…and the woman expected her to *stop*?

Luckily for Sally though, she wasn't the only one who'd dreamed of this sort of thing.

Having wished that she was the one on the receiving end of this abuse, Carol finally took the initiative and walked up beside the schoolmistress's chair, took her knickers down and waited politely for her turn. And spotting the girl out of the corner of her eye, standing quietly with her head bowed, her hands in her lap and her knickers around her ankles, Katie decided that a nice, fresh peach would be just the ticket, and pulled Sally back up on to her feet.

"Have you learnt your lesson?" she snapped, still holding the sobbing girl by the wrist.

"Yes, Miss," whimpered Sally.

"Then get your knickers down around your ankles, stand over there facing the scenery wall and leave your bottom on show."

As Sally almost tripped over her knickers in her eagerness to follow her wrathful colleague's instructions, Katie turned her attention to her next victim.

"Are you in need of some discipline as wel, my dear?" she asked commandingly.

Carol actually started to quiver with fright. Maybe this hadn't been such a good idea after all.

She was about to decline, when all of a sudden she found herself lying across Katie's lap and willingly confessing how very naughty she'd been.

"Well," beamed Katie with a crocodile smile, "we'd better make sure that you're better behaved from now on, hadn't we?"

And with her spanking hand now as good as new, Katie put the paddle to one side, pulled Carol's skirt up around her waist and began to smack each of her darling little cheeks in turn, as painfully and as delightfully as before.

"Oh please, Miss!" Carol wailed, milking the experience for everything it was worth. "I'm sorry! *Please* don't spank me any harder!"

"I'll decide what you deserve, my darling!" said Katie as she spanked the whiny little pup harder than ever. "And if you keep bawling like that, then I'm going to decide that you deserve a paddling as well."

"Please, Miss! No!" she screamed, struggling as hard as she could. "*Anything* but that!"

Having lost count of how many strokes Katie had taken across her cheeks, Carol finally decided that she'd had enough and fell silent to show that she'd learnt her lesson. But just as she let Carol up, Katie noticed two of the other schoolgirl extras standing with their heads bowed, their hands crossed in their laps and their knickers down around their ankles, patiently awaiting their turn.

Quickly packing a very tearful Carol off to stand facing the scenery wall beside Sally, Katie then pulled Tina across her knee and began all over again.

By the time Stacey had 'learnt her lesson', half the girls in the class were standing in line by her chair and waiting for their turn. And after the next girl had been disciplined, they all were.

Thirty well-tanned bottoms later, Katie rose from her seat and surveyed her handiwork: a whole class of tearful, sniffling girls, sore and humiliated with their pillar-box red bottoms on show, feeling too ashamed to even raise their heads.

It was clear that Katie had a talent as well as a taste for CP. Because despite having had more than an hour to recover, Sally and Carol were still as delightfully rosy as the last girl in line.

Tired and breathless, Katie seriously considered calling it a day and getting back to the script. But now that she'd the discovered the joys of a good, old-fashioned spanking, she wondered whether she might have been too quick to judge with the cane?

In any case, there was one sure way to find out.

"Turn around and face me girls!" She bellowed as she put away the chair and picked up the rod of willow for a second time, swishing it a little for dramatic effect. "Are there any volunteers or should I just pick one of you at random?"

About a quarter of an hour before the director was due to return, the whole theatre echoed with the sound of breaths being sucked through gritted teeth; the class trying to ease the pain of the throbbing welts that criss-crossed their bottoms.

Having already had a dose of willow that day, Sally was by far the most tearful of the group. But even so, once all of their bottoms had cooled a little and they had pulled their knickers back up, she was the first in line to thank Katie for the wonderful experience.

When Mary returned, she sat in the third row expecting to see the same old rubbish. But instead, she witnessed the most powerful stage drama that she ever could have imagined.

Katie was a complete tyrant who swung her cane so ferociously that it sent chills down the director's spine. Sally went from being a rebel without a cause to a girlie without her teddy bear, and the extras were all superb.

What was more, in some inspired ad-libbing, several of the girls tried to help Sally but ended up being thrashed and sent to the corner with their bare bottoms on display. The whole scene was tripled in length by the schoolmistress's insistence that every miscreant be spanked over her knee and paddled soundly before being caned. And the result was that the first scene was by far the longest and most riveting in the entire play.

At the end of the scene as the cast took their bows, Mary gave the most enthusiastic standing ovation of her career. She didn't know exactly what had happened in the three hours that she'd been away, but she thanked God that it had.

Despite Mary's sincere congratulations however, there was a sombre silence in the dressing room as the cast got ready to go home; the sadness that they would have to wait until tomorrow before they could rehearse again.

"You know," said Katie, "Mary may have thought that the scene was perfect, but I personally think that I could have done better."

"Yeah, me too," replied Sally. "I don't think that my terror was quite sincere enough when you told me to bend over."

"I suppose we *could* go back to my house and rehearse

some more?"

There was a moment's chattering amongst the extras before Carol was finally press-ganged into being their spokesperson.

"Erm, Katie?" she whimpered. "Would there be room for all of us as well?"

Him
by Cyanne

You know I want you, I've wanted you since the first time I saw you. It's rare, that kind of chemistry; it's not about being good-looking, or funny, or clever, or any of that, although you are all of those things. This is chemical, literally. It makes me feel a bit icky to say it as I don't want kids, but I guess on some primitive level I want your babies. But I don't want to dwell on that!

So … we fooled around, we became friends, you told me we could be nothing more. I know you love her and I don't want to take you away from her, but I know you want more, and I would be only too happy to give it to you. You feel guilty, sometimes you admit it, sometimes you don't, but I know you want me too. Just give in to it. I hold out hope that one day you will just give in to it. For years now, through other relationships, single times, other crushes, jobs, projects, interests … when it's time for my mind and fingers to wander, it's you. It's always been you.

We get a hotel. We hide our cars in different places just in case anyone recognises them. The sneaking around, the deceit, it's part of the fun. I know you love legs and shoes, so I'm wearing the tightest skinny jeans and heels. You've checked in and are already sitting at the bar when I walk in; you look me up and down and your eyes tear holes in me. I am weak with lust for you, more than any man I have ever met. I don't want to look like an escort and you don't want to look like a cheat, we agreed on the phone, so we peck on the cheeks and act like we're on a second date or something. Just being this close to you turns me on, the smell of your skin, the firmness of your body putting your arms around me. We have a drink and every movement, every comment, every flash of eye contact is loaded. You stroke my hair and it electric-shocks me. Our legs touch and I quiver. We were supposed to have dinner but we can't wait, we'll have to order room service later or something. You give me the room key and say you'll follow at a safe distance. We're not that far away from home, and you never know who's lurking around.

I strip down to my underwear, plain black strapless bra and thong with opaque, plain top hold-up stockings. My hair's black and my make-up's heavy and gothic, completely different to her and I know you'll love it. I keep my heels on. I throw a pink scarf over the lamp and put a CD on – Nine Inch Nails. She probably wants to fuck to Celine Dion or something. I'm going to be just the girl you want, which luckily is exactly the girl I am already. The hotel room's the perfect backdrop, just tacky enough, decorated in reds, perfect for adultery and filth and things never to be spoken of but often dreamed about.

I pile on even more make-up, light a cigarette and sit in the big black armchair. I resist the urge to touch myself; I'm already wet but I want your fingers, or – oh my god! – your tongue, to be the first thing I feel. When you come in I almost faint with lust, and I love the fact that I can see you react to me the same way. I take a long drag on the cigarette, looking you dead in the eyes.

You love going down on a girl more than anything, and you can't wait but I try to make you wait a little while. I know you'll be in control soon enough but it's more fun for you to break me if I'm strong. You kneel in front of me trying to pull my panties off and I tell you to wait until I've finished my cigarette. You start to play with my shoes, cradling my foot and stroking my insteps, held firm by the leather. This pulls my legs a little bit open and you tear your eyes away from my foot to try to make out the folds of my pussy under my thong. Stroking up my leg strongly with both hands you play with my stocking tops, staring hungrily all over my body. I'm enjoying the power, for now, but I'll relinquish it to you in time and you know that. You watch the cigarette going down, like an egg timer for when the roles will change. You kiss my shoes, my ankles and up my legs. At the top of my stockings you hesitate, before blowing, nibbling, licking my bare thighs. I moan as you press your lips to my cunt through my panties. You love female juices so much and you try to pull them aside but I wriggle away, pointing at the cigarette, and taking another drag. You can wait, and you go back to playing with my shoes, a look of fascinated innocence on your face.

I stub out the cigarette and start to submit to you. You motion for me to turn around and I kneel up on the chair, leaning forward over the back and sticking my ass out. You walk round me, admiring every angle, stroking my face as I stay resolutely prone, running your hands over the rounds of my buttocks and down the backs of my legs.

'You fucking temptress,' you say, not harshly, but with just a hint of aggression.

I stare ahead, the patterns on the curtains swirling as my eyesight starts to go wonky with lust, and hear you unbuckling your belt. I try to turn and you press my face into the chair with your hand. You stroke my ass and every time your fingers graze just a little bit closer to my pussy. The leather feels different to your hand, cooler and less pliant, as you stroke the belt down my back, over my ass, and down the backs of my legs. The contrast between the feminine gauzy stockings and the manly utility of the leather belt as they meet each other does it for me, and I know you know this.

The first smack with the belt is a surprise, not unwelcome, but harsh and shocking nonetheless. It smarts. My gentle female arousal is punctuated by the flat slap of the belt, right across my arse, and a low grunt from you as you do, loving hurting me, punishing me for tempting you, and loving that I love it. I arch my back up and lift my head, crying out – it does actually hurt, even though the rush and the turn-on are amazing. The music is getting particularly industrial and thrashy and you are getting into your stroke, and three harder smacks crash down on me, and I cry, eye make-up smearing down my cheeks, black lines of drama that lovers love.

My arse and the tops of the legs smart from the thrashing and you stroke me gently, sliding your hand over where the welts are just starting to appear. My pussy's gushing, aching for your touch. You slowly edge my panties down a little bit, which stings as they graze over my spanked buttocks. How do you know? How can you have the same, equal and opposite turn-ons to me? It's almost like I'm writing it, almost like you're reading my mind. You leave my panties stretched between my upper thighs – it's perfect, I love it. Kissing your way down my back you work your way down and I arch backwards, begging you with my body. You allow me just a few seconds, flickering your tongue into my cunt, wet with spit and pussy we squelch together and I'm spinning with lust, feeling like I'm about to faint.

You tell me to get on the bed and I obey. I want to obey you, and I know that by obeying you I am giving you what she won't, and it's so perfect. I am moving carefully, wobbling on my heels a little, my legs weak and my marks hurting. I go to pull my panties back up and you shake your head.

'You can take those down.'

So I do, stepping out of them, loving the abandon I feel. No knickers, hair aflutter, my shoes bondage in themselves as I struggle to control the high heels in my weakened state.

The bed is dark red, and flanked by a huge mirrored wardrobe down one wall. I lie on my back as you tell me to and touch myself between the legs. I could come in an instant if you'd let me but I don't think you're going to quite yet. You smile, shaking your head at me. You're trying to look harsh but you're loving this. You kneel on the bed and pull my legs up, over my head, almost into a shoulder stand, hooking the heels of my shoes under the top bar of the high metal headboard. I look at myself in the mirror, looking like a total porn star, a little narcissistic maybe but you love me for it – she doesn't even shave her legs.

My ass is lifted off the bed by my feet being hooked and you give it another whack with the belt, and another, and my heels take chunks of paint off the wall as I try to wriggle away from the pain. Then your fingers are on my pussy, one finger stroking up and down so gently and I'm almost coming. Then your tongue, and I'm coming against your face, screaming, sweating, not caring – the mirror showing a porno flick of a fully clothed man pressing his face into this total slut's cunt. But it's me. And it's you. It's you.

The French don't call it the little death for nothing. I am momentarily destroyed, unable to focus or think straight. And you are up beside the bed, your mind still clear, and you're undressing. Your body is perfect for me, muscular, tattooed; I love your strength and the contrast of you to me. I want you to hold me to your chest but you're pressing your cock into my mouth, pulling me up onto my knees so you can see in the mirror. I put on a show, arching my back and licking your cock and sucking just the end, locking your gaze in the glass. I can see your gaze travelling from my mouth around you, down my arched back, to my bare ass and the red marks before my stockings and those shoes. You love everything I love, and I suck you.

You want me on my back again, and I willingly comply. Again, my legs are up and hooked, and it aches, but it's worth it. You kneel over me, and gently now start to push into me, just the tip, and it drives me wild. I'm begging you to fuck me hard, but you're so in control, and that makes me even madder. I want you to lose control like I have, and we both know what's going on, and I love it. I'm so wet and you slide your cock around, getting it wet, and start to nudge it against my ass. I protest theatrically and you smile and carry on. I open up to you and you slide in further, your sudden gentleness both delicious and frustrating. You're rubbing my clit so gently, and moving the head of your cock in and out of my ass, and I'm going to come again. My wetness is trickling down and you're sliding in and out so gently, and my clit is swollen and super sensitive under your touch, and I'm coming, thrusting up to meet you and pulling you further into me, the mixture of sensations more than I can handle.

You pull out and wank over me, both of us watching each other in the mirror, and your cum showers me and you hold me tight, open and vulnerable just for the moment. Just for tonight.

Learning her Lesson
by Chloe Devlin

The click of the door sounded louder in the quiet room than it actually was. Debbie knew that the sound meant she was caught. And that she would be punished.

The Jenkins had told her their rules when she'd moved in at the start of her last semester in college. Staying out too late was a major no-no. And sneaking in was an even bigger one.

She pulled herself the rest of the way through the window into her room. As she stood up, a light flashed on, revealing Mr Jenkins standing in the doorway to her bedroom. He had a wooden instrument in his hand, kind of like a fraternity paddle.

"Where have you been, Debbie?" His deep voice sent shivers through her. So far she'd behaved well enough to escape punishment, although she'd heard the cries of some of the others when they misbehaved. Although no one would tell her exactly what happened behind closed doors, they always had a sparkle in their eyes the next day when talking about it. A spurt of excitement shot through her at the thought that she'd finally discover all those secrets.

"At a party, Mr Jenkins." Her voice quavered, despite trying to keep it steady. "I'm sorry I'm late."

He tapped the harsh wood against the palm of one hand. "I'm sorry, too, Debbie. You know you broke the rules."

She nodded, her heart starting to pound.

"Then you know you must be punished." The words slid against her skin like silk, arousing every nerve ending.

She shivered again, but didn't say a word as he locked the door behind him, his body a menacing presence. She knew he'd never seriously hurt her, but she also knew that she wouldn't escape punishment. She trembled as he walked over to her, but by clenching her fists, she managed to stay put when he reached out a hand to touch her shoulder.

"Take this off," he said, fingering the cotton material of her shirt.

She stared at him, wide-eyed. Did he really say what she thought? Was this really going to happen?

"You heard me," he said. "I want you to take off your blouse and skirt." He whacked the wooden paddle against his denim-clad thigh, the sound reverberating in the room. "Now!"

Feeling self-conscious, she slowly unbuttoned her blouse and drew it off her shoulders and arms. Then she unfastened her long, flowery skirt and let it drop to the floor. Thinking she might meet up with Ricky, she'd worn her nicest undies – her garter belt and stockings with matching bra and thong.

"The bra and thong, too," he said. "But leave the rest on."

Wondering what on earth was going on, she reached behind her and unsnapped the tiny hook holding her bra closed. It fell forward on her arms, letting her small breasts poke free. In the cool air of the room, her nipples puckered invitingly. But she also knew it wasn't entirely the cold that made them do that – it was also a deep-seated excitement that was building in her belly.

Mr Jenkins reached into his back pocket and withdrew two lengths of rope. "Hands out. Wrists together," he ordered.

She swallowed hard, but obeyed. He swiftly lashed her wrists together, intertwining the rope so there was no hope that she'd be able to free herself. Not that she really wanted to. The rasp of the rope against the inside of her wrists made her wonder what it would feel like looped around her thighs or even her tits.

She quickly obeyed his command to get on the bed on her knees and stretch forward. Without her hands, she fell forward, landing on her chest, the rough blanket like sandpaper against her hard nipples. She turned her head so that her cheek rested against the cover as Mr Jenkins took her bound hands and used the second piece of rope to secure them to the headboard.

"Spread your legs," he said.

She shuffled her knees sideways, trying to obey the best she could. With only her garter belt and stockings, she felt incredibly exposed. And with each inch that she spread her legs, her excitement built. Fresh air wafted over her pussy, making her aware that she was dripping with arousal.

"Wider." He tapped the inside of each thigh with the wooden paddle. "I want you stretched wider."

She kept shifting her knees apart until she thought her hips would pop. "Mr Jenkins, I –"

He ignored her hesitant words. "That's fine. Now you're ready. I'm not going to gag you. If you cry out or scream, I will. Do you understand?"

She nodded, the blanket harsh against her cheek. "I understand."

"Good. Now, I'm sure you've heard whispers and rumours about punishment in this house." He smoothed one hand over her taut buttocks, gently caressing. "Not only did you stay out late, but you were caught trying to sneak back in from a party. I have no doubt you went to this party to meet a boy. But if you're not responsible enough to be home on time, then you cannot be permitted to attend such functions."

"But ..." Her protest died off as he moved his hand to her other cheek, cupping and massaging her flesh.

"And I'm equally certain you went to meet this boy because you thought he could satisfy certain … urges you may feel. However, after tonight, I guarantee you won't care about meeting that boy because I'm going to satisfy those urges. Remember, no crying out." Before he finished the warning, he lifted his hand and brought it down on one side of her butt.

The sting shot through her body and she stiffened against the unexpected pain, her back going rigid. But she managed to keep from crying out, biting hard on her lower lip. Instinctively, she whimpered, "One."

"Oh, no, my dear," he said. "There's no need to count the number of strokes. The number doesn't really matter. It's all about the pain and the pleasure."

Both sensations collided in her gut as his blunt fingertips swirled around her cunt, parting her pussy lips and sliding through the slickness. She shivered and clenched her insides, trying to hold on to the sensations. Then another swat landed on the other butt cheek.

Debbie managed to keep from crying out each time Mr Jenkins' palm landed on her flesh. But it was getting harder and harder to contain her arousal as he touched her pussy or labia or clit after each swat. Keeping her hips still for the punishment, she wriggled her upper body, revelling in the roughness of the blanket against her nipples, sending an aching arousal coursing through her entire body. Another whimper escaped as she clenched her insides, wondering just how much of this pleasure and pain she could take.

"You're positively dripping," he crooned softly. "You must be full of those naughty urges. But don't worry, I'll take care of you."

She gasped as he thrust two fingers into her tight pussy.

Holding them deep inside her body, he continued spanking her ass, the slaps landing with a steadier rhythm. Just as she began to get used to the sensation, he wiggled his fingers inside her body. Then he thrust his fingers in and out of her pussy, like a hard dick fucking her.

Debbie thought she'd died and gone to heaven. Never in her wildest imagination had she ever thought something like this could happen to her. It made the things she'd done with Ricky seem positively tame and juvenile in comparison.

She knew that after tonight she wouldn't be seeing him again anyway. Compared to Mr Jenkins, Ricky was nothing more than a bumbling boy, fumbling around her body, unable to truly arouse her.

She began to move her hips forward and back, away from his insistent fingers and then back into each stroke of his palm against her butt. Back and forth, she established a hard-driving rhythm, wondering if this was what all the girls meant when they talked about coming so hard their brains exploded. She felt like she was going to fly apart if she didn't come pretty soon.

"Are you ready for a bit more?" Mr Jenkins asked.

"Please, oh, please," she whispered. "Everything. I want everything."

The rhythmic slaps stopped momentarily, although the insistent thrust of his fingers didn't let up. She tightened her pussy around the invaders, ratcheting up the sensations streaking through her body.

Then a harder, firmer smack landed against her blushing ass and the world came to a halt. His hot palm rested on her butt, pain blossoming from the spot it was touching. Two fingers had become three in that instant, stretching her, filling her.

A small cry escaped, half muffled by the blanket beneath her cheek.

"This is your only reminder," he warned. "If you continue to cry out, I'll be forced to gag you."

Silently swearing not to make another sound, she clamped her lips together, determined not to be gagged. As he wiggled his three fingers inside her pussy, he touched a place that was more sensitive than anything she had ever felt. Debbie jerked in response, feeling her pussy flood with a wetness she'd never experienced before. The breath whooshed out of her lungs and she gulped in as much air as she could.

The hand started swatting her again, a swift deliberate cadence that matched his finger-fucking tempo. The pain and pleasure mingled through her body, touching off fireworks in every nerve ending, especially throughout her pussy. "Oh, oh! Oh, yes! Please!" She begged him to make her come.

Every muscle in her body tightened as she soared towards her climax. She panted through the waves as he gave one final thrust of his fingers and one final smack of his hand. His thumb pressed hard against her throbbing clit and the pressure sent her over the edge.

Gasping for air, she arched her back. Her tits throbbed with sensation and her nipples felt like they would burst against the blanket. Her mind blanked out with the overpowering sensations. Finally she began to come down off her orgasmic high.

As her heart thudded in her chest, she realised she was still stretched out on the rough blanket with her knees spread bone-crackingly wide. Mr Jenkins still had three fingers buried deep inside her spasming pussy. He wiggled them again. "Ready for the second part of your punishment?"

Her eyes widened. There was more? She didn't know how much more her body could take. So much pleasure was fizzing through her veins like champagne, she felt drunk on the sensations.

Ed Jenkins chuckled to himself as he watched Debbie's expressive face. He'd been waiting weeks for the opportunity to discipline her. And now that it was here, he was going to enjoy it to the fullest extent. Her perky tits and ripe nipples poking through the tight T-shirts always called to him, crying out for attention. *For his attention.*

That would be the lesson next time. Taming her tits. But this time, it was her ass he wanted to blister. Her beautiful butt cheeks that he wanted red-hot and blushing beneath his hands.

He reached into his pocket for one final item. When he opened his hand, a pair of silver Ben Wa balls lay in his palm. Just the thing, he thought. With the way she had responded to his spanking and finger-fucking, she would go through the roof when he paddled her with these babies in.

He slowly withdrew his fingers from her cunt, trying to keep as much juice on them as possible so he could lube up the Ben Wa balls. When they were slick, he gently popped the first one in.

"Oh!" Surprise coloured her voice.

"One more, my dear," he said, nudging the second silver sphere into her tight hole.

"Oh, God!" she whimpered, but didn't break her position.

He smoothed his finger over her puckered hole, amazed that she had taken both balls so easily. No sign remained of the silver pleasure balls. The only thing visible was the wire leading to the control box. "We'll start off small and see what happens. Are you ready?"

"Ready for what?"

"To be paddled."

She swallowed, then squirmed as he turned the control box to the first setting. "I-I guess so."

He turned and picked up his old fraternity paddle. Who would ever have imagined the uses he would find for it? Certainly not his strait-laced frat brothers. They'd be having mini-strokes if they could see him now. And they sure as hell wouldn't have any idea what to do with the delectably blushing female bottom in front of him that clenched and unclenched as it waited for his paddling.

He brought the wooden instrument down on each cheek in turn, drawing a soft grunt from the girl. But no cries floated back to him. It pleased him that she learned so quickly. After a few more swats, he turned up the vibrations on the Ben Wa balls to the medium level.

He resumed his paddling as her hips started to weave back and forth. He licked his lips, imagining that he was plunging his rock-hard dick in between those red-hot cheeks, plundering her sweet ass. Behind the tight zipper of his jeans, his dick lengthened even more. But tonight wasn't about him or his dick. It was about punishing Debbie – and doing it in such a manner that guaranteed she would be craving his punishment for months to come.

Soft moans filled his ears as he continued the paddling. But her hips never stopped their movement. When she started a pumping movement, he increased the vibrations from the Ben Wa balls, flipping the switch to high. In between smacks, he could hear the whine of the balls, even snuggled deeply inside her ass. She raised her butt time and time again to his paddle, tiny grunts escaping from her with each smack.

He reached in between her legs, sliding his fingers along her puffy labia. Her juice coated his fingers as he played with her pussy.

"Oh, please," she whimpered. "Please, I need to come again."

"Do you think you've been punished enough?"

She twisted her head to the other side, her chest still

resting on the blanket. "I don't know. Please … just let me come."

He continued smacking her behind as he slid his fingertip farther, flicking her clit repeatedly. Her groans grew louder, more desperate. Finally, ready to give her another orgasm, he thrust his finger deep into her pussy, feeling her muscles tighten around him. "OK, Debbie. Come now!"

She let out a small cry, then collapsed against the bed, her entire body shaking with her orgasm. He stopped the paddling and withdrew his finger from her pussy, but let the Ben Wa balls continue buzzing away, each vibration multiplying until she arched her back again.

Debbie nearly cried with relief as the painful smacks of the paddle ceased. But the incredible vibrations from whatever Mr Jenkins had stuffed in her ass continued unabated. All she could do was squeeze her muscles tightly until she could squeeze no more. Several more strong spasms shook her body as she gulped in air.

The intensity waned as he slowly turned the control box to low. She gave a shuddering sigh, trying to come to terms with her complete abandoned behaviour. But all she could do was wait for her heart to stop pounding so loudly and her pulse to slow down. Mr Jenkins brushed back a strand of damp hair from her face. She opened her eyes, staring at him through a haze of pleasure.

"I hope you've learned your lesson."

Which one, she thought? The lesson to not come home late, or the one about deliberately coming home late so she could get more of this delicious punishment. She nodded.

"Good." He began to untie her hands from the headboard. "Just remember the consequences if you decide to stay out late."

"Oh, I will," she promised, with a secret little smile. "I will."

Sprung
by Deva Shore

My sister was having a sleep-over. It was her birthday and some of her girlfriends thought it would be a good idea to hire scary movies and make a night of it. They were all single and desperate. Loved nothing more than getting together and bagging guys.

A few bottles of wine always loosened them up and that's when the fun usually began. I loved listening to them crap on about their love lives or the lack of them.

I was twenty, two years older than Sheila, and I normally found her and her immature friends boring. The only time they really interested me was when they'd dare each other to do silly things.

One summer's night they dared each other to run down the street naked. I tried to capture them on my mobile phone but I was too far away and the images didn't come out.

Another time I snuck a look through the window and caught two of them French kissing while the others watched. Tonight I was hoping they'd go one step further, maybe get their gear off and fool around.

I'd slipped a lesbian porno in amongst their movies and made sure there was a gap in the curtains so I could watch from outside the window if anything interesting happened.

They thought they were alone and to be honest I was nearly ready to let them know I'd come home so I could go to bed. They were drinking a lot and so far hadn't seen the lesbian tape.

Finally Sheila picked it up.

'Who put this in here?' she giggled.

The girls crowded around oohing and ahhing. She slipped it into the machine and before long two of the girls were putting on their own exhibition.

The others openly fingered themselves as they watched. Me, I pulled my cock out and stroked it until I was shooting cum all over the garden. There was nothing better than being a Peeping Tom I decided after I made my way in.

'I'm home,' I yelled as I made my way to my room, wanting nothing more than a good night's sleep now that I'd had my fun, but someone was just coming out of the toilet and wouldn't let me pass. As my eyes adjusted I saw who it was.

'What were you up to?' Mary, Sheila's best friend, wanted to know.

'Nothing,' I mumbled, trying to ignore her as she blocked my way.

'You were watching us, weren't you?' she demanded, pushing me into my room and locking the door.

'Hey, what the hell do you think you're doing?' I said.

'You've been a bad boy, haven't you?' she demanded.

'No,' I said. 'I don't know what you're talking about.'

'Yes, you do.'

'It was you who put that tape in with Sheila's others, wasn't it?'

I smirked, couldn't help it. 'So what if I did.'

'Well, I think you knew that the girls would find it kinky and that you'd get your rocks off watching.'

'So what?'

'So, I think you should be punished for doing it.'

'You're nuts,' I said.

'I said I think you should be punished.'

'I'm not deaf. I heard you.'

'Well, then I think you'd better pull down your jeans and I'll have to give you a spanking.'

'You're kidding, right?'

'Wrong. I'm deadly serious.'

'Look, get out of my room, OK.'

'No.'

I made to move past her, to open the door and throw her out.

'Touch me and I'll scream.'

'Go ahead.'

'I'll scream rape.'

'You wouldn't dare.'

'Wouldn't I?'

We eyed each other. Mary wasn't bad looking; she had a great body, I'd just seen that. Great tits and arse. Sheila had looked as though she'd enjoyed going down chomping on her pussy so I thought what would it hurt. Let her give me a bit of a spanking and then she could go.

'OK, just hurry up and get it over with.'

'Good,' she giggled. 'Now step out of your jeans.'

I did.

'Hmm, nice,' she said, running her hands over my bum.

Her fingers worked magically as they ran over my cheeks, giving me a bit of a hard-on. I'm sure she noticed and now I felt uncomfortable as I thought she'd just give me a bit of a slap or two and be on her way.

'Very nice,' she said as her hand grazed my cock. She moved towards my writing desk and picked up a ruler and slapped it in the palm of her hand.

'You never said anything about a ruler,' I said.

'You never asked. Now come over here,' she said, sitting on my chair and patting her lap. 'Bend over my knee so I can give you that spanking.'

106

I felt really stupid doing it but I wasn't going to risk my sister's wrath if she went through with her threat and screamed.

I kneeled over her lap, my hands touching the floor.

She pulled my jocks down, exposing my bare arse.

'Hey,' I made to protest but a quick slap on my cheek shut me up instantly.

'No talking,' she insisted.

Her hand glided over my cheeks and the welt I'm sure the ruler left. Suddenly she slapped the other cheek with her hand, hard, real hard.

'Hey, that hurt,' I said.

'It's supposed to. Now be quiet.'

She ran her hand over my other cheek, rubbing it, and something happened, I don't know what. I found I was enjoying it. Enjoying lying over her with my arse up in the air, enjoying anticipating the next slap, wondering how much it would sting, if it would be the ruler or her hand.

The waiting became agony. I didn't dare speak. My cock was beginning to grow and she chuckled knowingly. A finger ran down the crack of my arse, over my puckered hole and down further to cup my balls.

As I was enjoying this the other hand let loose with a might slap of the ruler. The sting was so great I almost screamed out. Then there was another and another. It was as though my cheeks were on fire and then it was her hand slapping at me, a different type of pain as the sharp sting of her fingers over the welts almost brought me to tears.

Her hand wiggled between my thighs.

'Open them,' she demanded.

I did and she cupped my balls, squeezing them cruelly.

I froze, wondering what was coming next.

The ruler was rubbing up hard against the crack of my arse and without warning she smacked at my balls, the pain shooting through me like hot lava.

'Fuck,' I whispered as my breath expelled.

'Did you speak?' she demanded.

'No.'

'Good, I wouldn't want to have to give you another spanking.'

I said nothing but felt the beads of perspiration on my forehead pop.

'You can stand now,' she said.

I did and my erection stood out before me.

'You enjoyed that, didn't you?'

I wasn't sure what to say. I did enjoy it. Loved the way she made me feel as she took control over me, spanking and slapping at me.

'Step out of your jocks and remove your T-shirt.'

Oh, fuck. I thought all my Christmases had come at once. Now she was going to let me fuck her. I could barely contain myself.

Standing naked before her I watched her rise. Her pretty pink nightie, almost see-through, showed me what I'd seen earlier. Her gorgeous body.

'You like what you see?' she asked as she strutted before me.

'What?'

'My tits! You like them, don't you? Want to see more?' she purred as she undid the buttons halfway down, giving me quick glimpses of her pearly flesh.

'I … er …' Shit, I didn't know what to do. I was used to being the aggressor. For years now I'd been dominating the girls I took out. It was me who called the shots not some little friend of my sister.

She flashed her tits at me, opening and closing the fabric. She was hot all right and looked as though she knew what she wanted. I wasn't sure how to play this one so I thought I'd stall for time, see how it all turned out.

'I'll let you touch them if you want,' she said, coming

closer to me and practically rubbing them against my chest.

'I'm not interested,' I said.

She laughed. 'You've got to be joking. That's not what your cock's saying.'

She was right, of course, but I was still nervous about her threat.

Her fingers were roaming over my chest, then down the sides of me to my hips. They lingered there lightly touching my legs. Her fingers were like fire burning me wherever they touched.

'I think that …' I didn't want her to stop but thought I should at least make some sort of attempt at taking charge here.

'You think that you'd like your hand inside my panties, don't you?' she whispered, her breath fanning my face.

Jesus. She was so hot. She pushed her pelvis in towards mine, our mounds almost touching. Then she pulled back, allowing one hand to stray beneath while the other lifted her hem higher, allowing me a peek.

'Very nice,' I almost swooned as her fingers slipped through my pubic hair almost touching my rock-hard cock.

'Hold on to that chair,' she demanded, pushing me towards it.

Eager for her hands to be on me again I did as she asked.

'Spread those legs,' she demanded.

I did.

'Further.'

I did.

I was quivering with anticipation, desperate for another spanking that would hopefully even lead to some mind-blowing sex.

I heard her pull the curtain ajar and, peered over my shoulder to see my sister and her friends all laughing at me.

'So how do you like it?' Mary smirked at me.

I was dumbfounded for a moment, unable to move and then with my cock rock hard I pulled the curtain back, flushing with embarrassment as the girls applauded and jeered.

'I suppose you think that's funny,' I said.

'Yes, I do,' she said as she made her way to the door.

'Not so fast,' I said.

She turned.

'Now I think it's my turn to give you a spanking; after all, what you did was even worse than me.'

Her hand was on the doorknob and I saw the twinkle of desire in her eyes.

'I don't think so,' she said half-heartedly.

'I do. Now come over here,' I said, pulling her by the arm.

She came and I knew I'd won her, knew that if she could give a good spanking then she'd probably enjoy one just as much.

'Lie over my knee,' I said, sitting on the chair.

My erection had subsided somewhat but as she lay over me, her flimsy nightgown rising to show me her pretty panties, I felt it rise again.

I pulled her panties down, exposing her bare cheeks, and slapped at them. She flinched but didn't say anything so I smacked harder until I saw my handprints on her flesh.

'Oh,' she squealed as welts rose.

'You like that, don't you?' I said.

'Yes,' she whimpered.

'Open your legs so I can touch your pussy.'

She did.

My hand slid down the crack of her arse to cup her pussy. She was on fire. The heat coming from there was amazing. I slid a finger down her flaps, amazed to feel the wetness there already. She wiggled her bum at me encouragingly.

Slipping in a finger I marvelled at her silkiness, knew I had to have her and have her quickly.

'Get up,' I said. 'And take off your nightie.'

She did, stripping completely. Her nipples were hard. I tweaked them, giving them a hard squeeze, loving it when she squealed with pain. I pulled her closer, tugging at a nipple. She leaned forward as I took one in my mouth, rolling my tongue over it, and she moaned with pleasure.

My hand slipped down over her naked mound and onto her flaps. I parted them sliding in a finger, then another, enjoying the sensation of having her do exactly as I wished.

'On your knees,' I demanded. 'Now suck my cock.'

She sucked like a pro. I held her head, controlling the movements until I felt I was about to come.

'On my bed, legs open.'

As quick as a flash she lay before me, her legs splayed wide.

Picking up the ruler I slapped at her pussy, gently, not wanting to hurt her. Her hands slid down her breasts, over her stomach to her pussy. She opened her flaps and stared at me.

'Slap me with your hand,' she whispered.

Hesitantly I did.

'Harder,' she demanded.

I slapped at her pussy over and over again, watching as her juices oozed from her. Her clit hardened, doubling in size. I touched it, amazed at how hard it was slipping under my finger.

'Oh, rub me,' she begged.

I did and within seconds she was coming. Her body arched then shook as a massive orgasm exploded from her.

'Oh God, fuck me, will you.'

I didn't need to be asked twice. I speared my rock-hard cock into her deliciously hot pussy and fucked her like I've never fucked anyone else before.

111

We came clinging to each other, her nails raking down my back, taking half my flesh with them.

We lay together in the aftermath of great sex, the room heady with our scent, and I promised her that from now on whenever she was naughty I'd repeat the spanking for her.

I couldn't wait for her to be bad again, I can tell you.

The Governess
by Izzy French

"Follow me, Mademoiselle."

Angelique kept her head bowed as she followed Monsieur Leveque into his study. She could feel Cook's gaze on her back as the oak door slammed shut behind them. No doubt she had witnessed this summons many times before, although, for Angelique, it had come sooner than she expected. The justice would be summary, no doubt. He would dismiss her, and she would leave the house the same day. She had known what he was like before taking the position. His reputation as a hard taskmaster had preceded him. She knew of several governesses who had left his home within days, hours even, of having undertaken the task of teaching his two young sons. Some of their own volition, some dismissed. What each of them had in common was that they would not speak of what had occurred whilst they resided in his home. But Angelique was determined. She would not allow him to intimidate her. She had wished to avoid him, to work well with his sons, and gain experience as a governess.

Monsieur Leveque sat behind the oak desk in a high-backed chair. He was silent, contemplative. He did not invite Angelique to sit. She glanced around the library, certain she would show no fear. The walls were lined with leather-bound books. She had visited this room before, but not when Monsieur Leveque had been home, had opened cabinets, taken books down and turned the pages with care. She had even taken one or two back to her room. He was a man of taste. The titles were those read in the salons of Paris, she was quite certain. She had been impressed.

"My sons like you, Mademoiselle."

His voice was surprisingly soft.

"And why wouldn't they, Monsieur?"

He looked surprised at her boldness. Maybe previous governesses had been compliant, unwilling to stand up to him. But she knew she was a good governess, and that they were learning much with her. She would not be mistreated.

"Because, Mademoiselle, they have never liked a governess before now. And neither have I. But still, you are not perfect. There have been infractions. And there must be punishment. We must all learn that there are consequences for our actions."

Angelique gulped but didn't look away. That would be admitting her fear. She held her hands before her demurely and held his gaze. He was an austere-looking man, but his face wasn't without charm. There was much gossip in the surrounding area about his wife. That she had left and fled to Paris with a lover, leaving her husband and the boys behind. If this were true, it might account for his severe demeanour. His dark hair curled over his collar, and his moustache was neatly trimmed. He could be considered a handsome man; the planes of his face were regular. He dressed formally, and his clothes were well cut. She could tell he was appraising her in return, taking in her grey governess's dress, and her neat figure. She wondered what his wife looked like. Was she handsome too? Pretty? There were no portraits of her around the house for Angelique to judge. She had a fleeting thought about how it would feel for him to touch her, to rest his hand on her cheek. She pushed that thought away.

She drew breath.

"Punishment, Monsieur? You must be mistaken. And I was in the middle of a lesson with Serge and Charles. I must return to them. We were learning about the Americas. They will spoil their work if I am gone from them for too long. They can be disobedient, at times."

She knew she was taking a chance, criticising his sons. But she felt the only way to gain respect, and keep her place, was to be honest with him.

"Cook is sitting with them, for now. The boys tell me you allow them to talk during mealtimes."

The tone of his voice had altered slightly. Still soft, it had an edge to it, something she was unable to grasp. Was her punishment to be dismissal?

"We talk of our day together, Monsieur. Of what we have seen on our rambles, for example. How we translate our observations to paper the next day. It is all productive, I assure you."

Her voice trailed away as he rose from his chair and walked to the corner of the room, where a riding crop rested against a wall. Her eyes widened. The boys had spoken to her of the punishment he meted out to them, on occasion. Across their hands. Surely he wasn't going to mete out the same punishment to her? A grown woman in his employment. How would she face his sons with marks across her hands? How would she ever make them obey her again? She flushed.

"I have rules, Mademoiselle. You were made fully aware of them when you accepted the post. And my rules must not be broken. I do not accept disobedience from my sons, or from my servants. Over here, please."

Angelique stayed exactly where she was. And she stayed silent.

"If you prefer, Mademoiselle, I could dismiss you. But I believe your family is in great financial need. I believe it would not sit well with them if you were to be summarily dismissed and returned to them, penniless and without references, would it? I know your father well. He is a proud man."

Angelique knew Monsieur Leveque was correct. Father was proud. He had once been a wealthy man, but had lost much money in an ill-fated adventure in the West Indies. Once he had moved in the same circles as Monsieur Leveque, but no more. He would be most displeased if Angelique were to return home so soon. He had entreated her to work hard.

"And, Mademoiselle, I would ensure you would never work as a governess again in this town."

His voice was raised now. He lifted the crop and whipped it against his desk. Angelique could see grooves there, where it had been whipped before. For the benefit of his sons, or other governesses? she wondered. She could not afford to lose her position, so she walked over to him, remaining upright and proud as she did so. He would understand she was not going to submit to a lashing willingly. He would know of her displeasure. He paid her wages, but he did not own her. She stood before him now, her face defiant. He breathed deeply, heavily. He flexed the crop, and stroked it against the palm of his hand. She waited for him to ask her to hold her hands out before her for him to hit them. She closed her eyes. If the pain became too intense she would make her thoughts wander. But that did not happen.

"I can see why my boys are so fond of you, Mademoiselle." He stroked the tip of the crop down her cheek, and across her shoulder to the lace edge of her dress. He traced a line down to her décolletage. She shivered. This was unexpected. But not unpleasant. In fact, she felt a tiny frisson of what she could only describe as excitement. He plucked at a ringlet that fell to one side of her ear with his left hand, and tugged slightly. The sensation was strange, a mixture of pain and sweetness.

"You are pretty. And clever. I can see that you understand me better than the others. They would have fled by now."

Angelique wasn't sure she agreed, that she did understand him, but she didn't demur. Then he stroked the cane over the surface of her dress, down her sleeve, round her waist and across her skirts, lifting the edge, showing the whiteness of her petticoats.

"Pretty ankles can tempt a man, you know."

She could have protested that if he hadn't lifted her skirt, exposing them, that they wouldn't have tempted him. That her ankles weren't routinely on show. That he had allowed himself to be tempted. She hadn't shown herself off. But she didn't speak.

"And I believe there have been other transgressions. I hear from my sons that you have taken books from my library, without my permission. You are a learned young lady."

Angelique dropped her head. So he knew about the books. The boys had told him, despite her express wish that they wouldn't. She had to have the books. Life in the house could be dull. She loved teaching the boys, but she soon grew bored of the tittle-tattle amongst the servants in the kitchen, where she was expected to spend her time when she wasn't teaching. She was drawn back to the present when she felt the crop begin to rise up her calf. Momentarily she had to suppress a giggle. The situation seemed entirely absurd. Then it snagged on her stockings and caught her skin. She gasped. It was as though he could read her thoughts.

"I will return your books to you, Monsieur."

"Indeed you will, Mademoiselle. But before you do, I would be grateful if you would bend over my desk. Now please." His voice was insistent. It brooked no argument. She met his eyes one last time, then turned from him and, bending at waist height, she rested her palms on the desk. Her chest heaved. She hoped he could not see her agitation. The crop was moving slowly up underneath her petticoats, reaching her thigh. Then his left hand picked up her petticoats and skirt and threw them up over her back, exposing her undergarments. Resting the crop against the desk, his hands roved over her backside. She shivered in anticipation, as the cool cotton rubbed against her skin. Then his hands reached between her knickers and tore them further apart. She stifled a protest, that they were handworked, by her mother, part of her going-away gift.

She pressed her legs tight shut. Perhaps she was deserving of this punishment. She had taken his books, after all, fully intending to return them, of course. And they had made interesting reading. She felt his lips brush across her skin. She closed her eyes. The feeling was exquisite.

"Are you ready, Mademoiselle?"

She did not answer him, nor give him any sign she had heard him. Her punishment would come whether she did so or not. And, although she felt powerless to resist the physical punishment, by refusing to communicate with him, she retained her dignity, and, with that, some power of her own. She waited. The crop whistled through the air administering the first blow with a sharp sting. Angelique squeezed her eyes tight shut. It hurt more than she anticipated. But as he raised the crop again the place between her thighs began to tingle with anticipation. She had to resist raising her arse to him. She would not show him her reactions.

The second blow came. Across both buttocks. The agony was soon becoming sweet, and the corresponding sensation between her thighs was intensifying. She had to resist the desire to reach down and satisfy that ardour as he whipped her. It was ironic, really. Often, alone in her room, with the books she had taken from the library, reading of such punishments, she would explore that part of herself that gave such sweet pleasure, bringing on waves of comfort that she had never known before. And now, in turn, she was receiving the pain and pleasure that was described within their covers.

Another blow came. He was relentless. She groaned. Her skin was becoming hot and sore. She twisted and turned her hips, writhing against the desk. He bent to her, kissing her skin again. She cried out.

Then he laid the crop beside her on the desk. She wished to take it up and turn and strike him in return, to see how he reacted, to see how it felt to lash his skin. But then some delicate, invisible thread hanging between them would be broken.

"I think that is enough punishment, for allowing my sons to talk at mealtimes, at least. Stand up."

Angelique was confused. Why was he stopping now? She was disappointed. She stood, allowing her petticoats and skirt to fall, skimming her burning buttocks. She winced. They stood facing one another in silence. Angelique wondered if she was to be dismissed from his company now. She would have to return to her room, unfulfilled. And then be forced to satisfy herself. Anger rose in her throat.

"But there is also the other matter. I have not yet punished you for stealing my precious books."

"I borrowed them, Monsieur. I will return them immediately. As soon as you release me."

"I am fearful for you, Mademoiselle. Fearful of your morality. If you would steal from your employer, when you are so new to his employ, to what moral depths would you descend?"

"I am good, Monsieur."

119

"That goodness needs testing, Mademoiselle. And reinforcing. Closer, please."

Angelique stepped towards him, not allowing her eyes to draw away from his gaze. Once she was within arms reach he grasped her, and in one swift movement, sat in his chair and threw her over his knee. Again he threw her skirts up. Angelique offered no resistance. She wondered what implement he would use this time. She was beginning to believe she deserved her punishment. She knew she was deriving pleasure from it, although she wished to hide this fact from him. And he would be deriving pleasure too, if he shared the sentiments she read about in his books, which he almost certainly did.

She was surprised to feel the palm of his hand strike her this time. His hand felt cool against her stinging buttocks, but his slap felt hard against her smooth skin. He raised his hand again and let it fall. Angelique twisted and squirmed within his grasp.

"I think this excites you, Mademoiselle." His voice was stern. She smiled down at the floor.

"No, Monsieur," she attempted to protest.

"I believe there is a moistness there, between your thighs. A moistness that usually demonstrates a woman's lust."

He traced his fingers over her buttocks before slapping her again, several times. His strike was firm and steady. He had done this before. She quivered with desire.

"You are a whore, Mademoiselle, to derive pleasure from my actions."

Angelique did not reply, but pushed her arse against his hand, willing him to delve between her thighs and satisfy her.

The next slap was electrifying. She groaned with longing, feeling helpless. Pressing herself into his lap she could feel that he, in turn, was excited.

"I see my punishment has inflamed you, Monsieur," she gasped, unable to suppress herself.

"You are very perceptive, Mademoiselle."

Instead of striking her this time, he rubbed her bottom, parted her buttocks and inserted several fingers deep inside her, thrusting for several moments, then pulled them from her. She felt her cunt tighten and release. She wanted him inside her now. He bent over her, kissing her buttocks, running his tongue over the lines left by the crop, the marks left by his hand.

"You taste sweet," he whispered. Her desire raged at the melting together of pleasure and pain. Pulling herself up, she twisted round on his lap, straddling him, allowing herself room to unfasten his trousers and release his cock. It was his turn to groan. Raising herself slightly, she tilted backwards and lowered herself onto his cock, feeling it nudge into her cunt, its passage eased by her juices. He threw his head back, having now surrendered herself to him. He held her hips and rocked her backwards and forwards, and they settled into a rhythm. Her buttocks rubbed against the serge of his trousers and the soreness felt exquisite. She felt his hand push itself between her lips, seeking out the tiny nub that so often afforded her pleasure when she was alone. He rubbed it firmly, encircling it with his finger as he thrust deep inside her, and she forced herself down on him in return. Their coupling was ardent, the fulfilment of the agonies of her punishment. He groaned as he reached his orgasm, and she soon followed him, waves of pleasure flowing through her cunt, all the more rapturous for what had preceded it. It took some moments for her to return to her senses, and she felt herself blush as they looked at each other, neither speaking. Her cunt still pulsed around him, her body still taking pleasure from his cock.

Before she'd had a chance to wriggle away from him,

he moved his hands to her bodice and tore it apart, revealing her small, firm, rosebud breasts. Her nipples were tight, hard with desire. He took one, then the other into his mouth, sucking, biting, scratching them with his fingers. She could feel herself begin to respond to him again, and felt his cock harden in turn too. She decided, though, that they had pleasured each other enough for today, and standing back from his lap, Angelique allowed her skirts to fall to the floor. He reached for her, thrust his hand back under her petticoats and slapped her thigh through her torn knickerbockers, but she stepped out of his reach. He sighed.

"I have never gone this far before with a governess, Mademoiselle," he said, sounding regretful. "You are extremely disobedient. Much more so than any of the others. You may leave now."

She nodded at him, then left the room, smiling, holding the torn fabric of her bodice to her chest, hoping to avoid the other servants as she returned to her room. She now knew where the power really lay between them. He had tested her. And he had also proven that he needed her. He would do this to her again. Of that she was certain.

The Rose
by Beth Anderson

Almost as soon as I arrived, I was naked. It was how he
wanted it, and how he told me it would happen. Only a few
minutes ago I'd nervously knocked on his door and walked
into the hall. I was to arrive in a black pencil skirt, black
seamed stockings, black heels and a white blouse, and
nothing else. "Underwear won't be needed," he'd already
informed me. "You know what to do" were his only words
as his fingers held my arms and he kissed me on the cheek.
You see, I'd been naughty and had confessed to him during
one of our many intimate chats that I'd been seeing lots of
men for sex. After this admission, he told me I was to
attend a 'training session'.

My heart was almost in my mouth as I stood in front of
him, slipping off my shoes, undoing my blouse and
exposing my breasts in front of him for the first time. I
thought about how different relationships are on the
Internet. That you can get to know someone so intimately
and yet have never met ... Unzipping my skirt and sliding it
over my thighs, I stepped out of it as demurely as I could. I
just hoped he'd not see how wet I'd become already, even
on the drive over here. I rolled the stockings down my
smooth legs and over my feet, placing them on top of the
rest of my clothes on the hall chair. I stood in front of him
and he took me all in. His eyes running up and down my
body, over my breasts and stomach, my waist and legs, and

123

examining my pussy. The tiniest smile appeared on his lips as he obviously noticed my wetness and he moved one hand towards me. A single finger traced a gentle line over me and slid inside me. I hid a little gasp as well as I could, but he just looked deep into my eyes and ran his wet finger over my red lips.

"You know what will happen tonight, don't you?" he asked me. I'd been fantasising about this moment for the last two weeks; I needed this to happen to me. I quietly replied, "Yes, sir." "Good," he answered, taking my hand. He led me through the hall and into his playroom with dim lighting and wonderful incense burning. The centre of the room held a large bed with black satin sheets and a single red rose in the centre. He'd already told me to expect a rose; it was for me to remember this night. All around was a collection of his various benches and furniture. I realised then that this was real. It was all going to happen as he said. Laying me down on the bed, he told me to close my eyes and relax. He walked purposefully around the room, arranging his implements and enjoying my naked presence.

Soon he was back at my side with leather restraints with large D rings at the sides of them. Both of my wrists and ankles were bound in these restraints and I was led to the first bench. Although very comfortable, I was aware that while I was being restrained to it, it pushed my hips upward and opened my legs; I could feel the cool air on me, almost as if I were on display for him. A flogger was placed on the bench in front of me, along with a crop, a paddle and a cane. He liked to do that; to show you how you would be punished before you received it. I relaxed into the bench feeling so very secure. I closed my eyes and took a long, slow breath.

His hands started to caress my naked bottom, stroking and kneading me. Slow, deliberate spanks started to rain down onto my willing behind and I let out a long, low moan. He picked up momentum, and the room was filled with the 'smack' sound of his hand, hard on my softness. I felt my bottom shake with every stroke and relaxed into his punishment, the glorious heat and redness building up. Each stroke seemed to go right through me, and I could feel my entire body responding to his hand. Right then and there, we were one.

The flogger came next and he expertly wielded it as each stroke shook me with its weight. Speeding up and slowing down, he was silent as he concentrated on delivering me the pain I needed. The sound of a flogger alone is enough to excite me, but his exquisite punishment was sending me to another world. Images of him holding me tight, inside me and looking into my eyes flashed through my mind as the intensity increased. Slowly I drifted to a place where only this moment existed. I forgot who I was and as the endorphins rushed through my body I cried out, a visceral and long cry.

I kissed the heavy black leather paddle as he held it in front of me. This was one of his favourites and was used only when he knew he had a very willing submissive. Placed on my red behind, it felt so cool and soothing. He gently ran its entire surface over me, enjoying my curves. With no warning he brought the paddle down onto me hard, once on each cheek. I was expecting a pause until the next stroke, but I should have known better. Stroke after stroke hit me, with the most almighty sounds. Each stroke rocketing through my entire body and making my fingertips tingle. As he continued spanking me with this wonderful implement, I started to wiggle and lift my feet up. I couldn't take any more. Tears were rolling down my cheeks as I screamed and shouted, cried out and thrashed in vain, strapped to the bench as I was. More and more it hit me, over and over. It seemed to get harder and harder as he found his rhythm and brought the paddle down onto me hard. I needed this so much and was swimming with pleasure, not aware of time or anything around me. But there was more, and more. When I thought I could take no more, there was. When I thought I was finished, I wasn't. He knew what I needed and he was going to enjoy giving it to me. Tears rolling down my face; I cried, screamed and breathed through each shuddering jolt.

Slowing down, he gently started to run his hands over me, examining his handiwork.

Without a word, the paddle was put aside and the cane was selected. That tiny, fragile thing that would cause me so much pain. I marvelled at its simplicity and purpose. "You will receive ten with the cane." He spoke in a soft and firm manner that didn't break the spell I was under, and I simply replied, "Thank you, sir."

I was to count each stroke and reply with "thank you, sir" after each one. The swishing sound that the cane made through the air as he warmed up was so intense that I jumped each time I heard it. I knew what was coming. A swoosh and the briefest of pauses and then a firework burst of pain jumped through me like a shock. I gasped and, composing myself, replied, "One, thank you, sir." I made sure I was as relaxed as possible throughout my caning so I might get through it. Each stroke was more painful than the last, but stroke after stroke, I counted and thanked him each time.

At the tenth stroke he paused. "This is your final stroke," he informed me, his firm and calm manner relaxing me. I heard the loud swish, and the cane met me; a millisecond pause and then pain erupted from deep within me. I screamed; from the deepest part of me, I screamed. Electricity shot through my body until I slumped onto the bench. Trying to get my breath, I was only aware of the burning line across my delicate bottom. I relaxed, smiled and wept ...

No Smoking
by Stephen Albrow

It was cold and dark, but Carly still went outside. She was the only smoker on the evening shift and there was no way she could survive her tea break without a couple of Marlboro Lights. She wished she'd brought her jacket with her, because her short skirt and blouse did little to protect her from the chill night air. But at least the ciggies would warm her up, if she could only manage to get them lit.

There was a disused doorway at the back of the office car park where the smokers huddled when the weather was bad. There was very little draft there, so Carly snuck inside, put a fag in her mouth and then sparked up her lighter. She felt a pleasing wave of relaxation, as the tobacco caught alight and the first plume of smoke billowed into her face. Working in a call centre could get stressful at times, with all those angry customers shouting down the phone, so she needed these moments of respite and calm.

Carly took a long draw on her cigarette and sent a long jet of smoke spiralling into the air. It caught on the breeze and dispersed in seconds, but not before someone had managed to spot it. And whoever it was, they appeared to be angry.

"Hey, you shouldn't be smoking there!" yelled a voice, and then a torch light shone in Carly's face. She froze for a moment, remembering all the times she'd been caught having a crafty fag in her lunch breaks at school, and feeling like a bad girl, she quickly stubbed the cigarette out and then hid her lighter down her cleavage crack.

And then she remembered she was an adult now and wondered why she'd reacted like that.

"But everyone smokes here," she said, as she saw the stranger getting closer. Only it wasn't a stranger. It was only Tim, the new security guard who had started last week. The young guard. The handsome guard. The one who looked cute in his uniform.

He stepped into the doorway and switched off his torch. They were close enough now for him not to need it. He sniffed the air and smelled the smoke, then shook his head in what seemed like disgust. But Carly couldn't tell if he was being serious or not. She was too busy thinking how sexy he looked when he was angry.

"Don't you read the notice board?" he asked, a hint of aggression in his voice.

"Why?"

"Because the rules have changed. You can't smoke anywhere within the office grounds now."

"I'm sorry," said Carly, looking down at her feet. There was something about the tall, muscular guard that kept making her feel like a naughty schoolgirl. Maybe it was the authority his dark blue uniform gave him, or the fact he was just so incredibly good-looking, or just his masterful way of speaking to her.

"Well, sorry isn't good enough, I'm afraid," said Tim, then he told her to turn around and face the wall. "I'm going to have to frisk you."

"You're joking, aren't you?"

"Do I look like I'm joking?"

Carly looked and he didn't. Unless ... Unless ... She stared into his big blue eyes and was that a twinkle in the corner of each? And that frown on his lips, that James Dean sneer, was there maybe a hint of a smirk about it?

"Face the wall," he yelled before she could decide, and he spoke with such force that she daren't disobey him. She turned to the wall and spread her arms and legs, then felt his warm hands upon her hips. He slid them up the sides of her torso, then ran them along her outstretched arms, his touch both firm and reassuring. This must have been what it would feel like to be frisked by a proper policeman. A little bit scary, but also quite exciting – especially the way it made her feel like such a naughty girl.

"What are you looking for?" she asked, as Tim's warm hands moved back along her arms and then back down to her hips.

"Evidence," he said, then he dropped to his knees and ran his fingers down the sides of her miniskirt.

"Evidence of what?"

"Evidence that you're a bad girl," Tim said, his hands now touching Carly's stocking-clad thighs. She looked down over her shoulder at him, wondering if he could see her stocking tops. The breeze kept ruffling the hem of her skirt, which only covered them by an inch or so.

"Well, you won't find nothing down there," said Carly, as Tim's hands ran right the way down her legs. She didn't mind him looking, though, because his touch felt even nicer through her soft, sheer nylons, and as his fingertips reached her shiny stilettos, she felt a tingle of arousal between her thighs. He had touched almost every inch of her body, and still his hands were on the move, sliding back up her thighs and then reaching round her body to search her stomach area and then her breasts. And that was the most thrilling moment of all, because that's where Carly had stashed her lighter. And it made her feel like such a bad, little girl – one who was about to be caught red-handed.

"Well, what have we here?" Tim asked aloud, as his fingers cupped the bad girl's breasts. He could feel the lighter through her silky blouse, but seemed far more interested in Carly's nipples. They were pert and hard, which might have been the cold, but Tim felt certain it was more than that. Carly's heart was beating fast and her cleavage was trembling, both obvious signs of how aroused she was.

"I'm going to have to confiscate this," Tim said, unbuttoning Carly's blouse and reaching inside. He squeezed her breasts through her lacy bra, then plucked the lighter from its hiding place.

"You can't," said Carly.

"I can," said Tim; and Carly still couldn't tell how serious he was, but if this was just Tim's way of flirting with her, then she liked his way of flirting a lot. Her body was tingling in all the right places – all the places he had fondled in the full and thorough frisking. And there was something about that uniform, too – it made her feel like she had no choice but to obey Tim's orders, no matter how ridiculous they might have seemed.

"You can't take the lighter, it's mine," insisted Carly, though she knew he could do whatever he liked.

"I'm taking it," he shouted, getting firmer with her now.

"But I'm a fully grown woman."

And that made Tim laugh.

"A fully grown woman?"

"Yes, I'm twenty-six years old," said Carly.

"Well, then why are you acting like a naughty little girl?"

"I'm not."

"Yes, you are. You've been caught smoking where you shouldn't have done. And that makes you a very bad girl – a very bad girl who needs to be punished."

And before she could put up any more of a fight, Tim hitched up the back of Carly's skirt. He smiled when he saw her stocking tops and then her black suspenders and her lace-trimmed knickers. They were clinging tight to her small, round buttocks, the fabric wedged between her cheeks. For Tim, it made an irresistible sight – such a perfect arse simply had to be spanked!

"You bad, bad girl," he muttered, keeping the skirt raised with one hand while lifting his other hand into the air. Carly closed her eyes. She could tell what was coming, but couldn't quite believe it was really true. She had never been spanked – not even at school – no matter how badly she had misbehaved or how many times she'd been caught with a crafty fag in her hand. No, she'd never been spanked, although she'd often deserved it, and so she couldn't wait to feel Tim's hand on her flesh.

She gasped, as his arm flashed through the air and the palm of his hand smacked into her arse. He'd caught her right in the middle of her plump left cheek, and though the thickness of her knickers had softened the blow, the mild twinge of pain was like a statement of intent – it was clear there was still much more to come. The second smack followed just a second later and was delivered with almost twice the force, confirming that the first strike had been nothing more than a warm-up blow. Crisper and harder, the second strike seemed to summon an instant bruise to her cheeks. She could picture her flesh turning all red and sore, as the pain it triggered made her buttocks throb.

"This'll teach you," said Tim, as he drew back his hand and then drove it hard into Carly's behind. Two blows came in quick succession – a smack to the left cheek and a smack to the right – and Carly yelled from the bitter sting now building up with each new thwack. Her cheeks were getting redder and sorer, with tender welts rising all over her arse, and as more blows came, now directed at these sore spots, the level of intensity made her tremble inside. It was such an overwhelming feeling – being made to lean over while her arse was spanked! It was painful and sore, and yet, despite all that, Carly pushed out her buttocks like she wanted more.

"Bad girl," said Tim. He had noticed her sticking her bottom out, and so he punished her with the hardest spank so far. "You're not meant to be enjoying this!" But Carly couldn't help herself. The constant throbbing in her bum cheeks was proving to be even more relaxing than a cigarette, because every spank seemed to wipe away any trace of guilt she had ever felt in the whole of her life. All the naughty things she'd ever done were now being punished. She was making amends for all her bad girl ways.

"Spank me harder," she said, and Tim rose to the challenge, delivering five quick strikes to Carly's left cheek. There was genuine aggression in every smack, like he was angry with her for wanting a harder spanking. Without really meaning to, she had put into question his dominant force, and so he now sought to teach her an even harsher lesson. To this end, he pulled her knickers down and began to spank her naked buttocks, determined to make her rue the day she had asked him to spank her with greater force.

Again and again, with increasing venom, the palm of Tim's hand struck Carly's cheeks. She was surprised by the difference being knickerless made – it was only a thin layer of silk after all – but without this, the smacks felt ten times harder and caused her to scream out loud with pain. The whole of her buttocks had turned red by now and so each new blow struck tender flesh, the whirlwind of slaps enflaming the welts and bruises already raised by Tim's firm hand. There was only so much of this a girl could take, and Carly felt close to reaching her limit. But then two things happened that changed her mind. First, her buttocks went numb, and then her cunt started throbbing.

Or had her cunt been throbbing for quite some time? It

was difficult to say with her arse cheeks aching. Tim's hand had made them sting so much, she'd been blinded to all other feelings in her body, but now he'd spanked them completely numb, she was able to feel the other effects of the fierce chastisement. A pleasing warmth was coursing through her body, which she assumed to be an endorphin rush, since it seemed to deaden any last trace of pain, while at the same time triggering a fiery sexual glow inside her. Beads of hot moisture wet the lips of her pussy, and she pushed out her arse cheeks once again. But this time she wasn't encouraging Tim to spank her even harder. Instead, she rubbed her bum against his crotch.

"Christ, you really are a bad girl," said Tim, who'd been gearing up for another firm strike. "I'm trying to teach you a lesson here."

"Well, there are others way of doing that."

"Like what?"

"Like fucking some sense into me!"

Carly's buttocks were still pressed tight against Tim's crotch and she could feel the firm, hard outline of his prick. It was bulging with the pent-up sexual tension that had been building inside him throughout the spanking, so she knew he wouldn't need much encouragement to start fucking her hot, wet pussy instead.

"Nice idea," said Tim, unzipping his trousers and then steering his hard-on between Carly's thighs. She was still standing in the frisk position, leaning up against the wall with her feet apart, which allowed him to enter her at speed from behind, his hands now gripped around her waist. She screamed as his manhood tore through her muscles. He had delivered the first thrust with so much force, Tim still seemed determined to teach her a lesson – it was as if he was still spanking her.

"Bad girl," he said, as he pulled back his hips and then powered his manhood straight back home. His full length entered Carly's pussy, sparking a wave of fierce convulsions in her clinging cunt walls. The spasms made her pussy feel twice as tight and forced Tim to increase the force of his thrusts, but the tall, strong, athletic, dominant guard was fully equipped to raise his game. Fuelled by a mixture of testosterone and adrenaline, he rammed his cock in and out of Carly's gash, loving how his thrusts were making her scream even louder than the firm, meaty spanks he'd given her arse.

"Are you learning your lesson?" he yelled in her ear, as he drove his dick through her slit. But such was the level of friction inside her, and so strong were the continual waves of tension in her cunt, that she could barely even remember what the lesson he wanted to teach her was, except it was something to do with her being bad – being bad and needing punishment. But this certainly didn't feel like a punishment to her – the non-stop thrusts of Tim's hard dick were making her insides shudder, her nipples throb and her body feel aglow like never before. He had stoked up a pre-orgasmic fire inside her, which sent jets of warm juice gushing down her thighs, and now her arms and legs began to tremble. She was almost there. She was almost coming.

It probably made no difference that Tim reached for her breasts and gave Carly's nipples a sudden tweak. The tension inside her had already gone past that point – that point where she could hold it back – and now her cunt muscles churned around his dick and the juices from her pussy ran faster and thicker. She threw back her head and roared with pleasure, then she felt his cock surge through her again, and with her walls now gripping skin-tight to his phallus, she could feel how close Tim was to a climax. His helmet was bulging at split-second intervals, the throbs sparking shivers in Carly's cunt. And then he pulled right back to the entrance of her pussy, ready to deliver a last, fierce thrust.

Carly let out another wild roar of delight, as Tim's full length hammered through her climactic walls. She felt his helmet pulsing deep inside her, as it showered her insides with jets of hot spunk. The jism struck her with surprising force. She could feel each bulge of Tim's helmet quite clearly, and when he thrust again to drain his balls completely dry, she felt the first rush of climax all over again. A new wave of spasms made her cunt muscles ripple and a fresh wave of juice spilled out of her slit. But better still than those two things was the sudden sense of relaxation she felt. Because Tim had done more than just fuck her that night – he had also corrected her bad girl ways. And that's why her buttocks felt so red and sore!

Tim gave them a slap just after withdrawing, reawakening the welts and bruises on her flesh. She felt a satisfying tingle of pain in her cheeks, which acted as a reminder of the lesson she'd been made to learn. She was not to smoke in the office car park. And the message could not have been hammered home more clearly by the dominant security guard who'd spanked and fucked her so forcefully. She turned to face him and saw him reaching in his pocket. She wanted to thank him for correcting her errant ways, but the words got stuck in the back of her throat.

"What's up with you?" Tim asked, as he pulled out a packet of cigarettes, took one out and then sparked it up.

"You're lighting up!"

"Of course, I'm lighting up. I always smoke after having sex."

"But you said this was a No Smoking area."

"Yeah, well, that was sort of a little white lie."

"A lie?" Had she just heard him right?

"Yeah, I sort of made the whole thing up. I suppose it was rather naughty of me, but then I've always been a very bad boy."

"You can say that again," said a dumbfounded Carly. "You're a very, very bad young man, indeed."

"So, does that mean I need a good spanking, Miss?" Tim asked, with a mischievous grin on his lips.

It was a naughty suggestion but Carly rather liked it. It would be fun to turn the tables on him.

"Yes, it does," she said, immediately getting into character. "So report back here tomorrow night, at nine o'clock sharp, and don't be late."

"Yes, Miss," said Tim.

"Oh, and Tim," added Carly, "I'm going to have to confiscate your cigarettes."

"Oh, Miss!"

"Hand them over!"

She was gasping for a fag now, so she snatched the packet and her lighter from him and lit one up. A quiet cigarette was what she'd come outside for in the first place, and as she took the first puff, she felt a need for peace and solitude.

"Dismissed," snapped Carly, and the naughty schoolboy daren't argue. He skulked away into the darkness. But he'd be back again tomorrow – she was certain of that! And this time it was *his* arse that was going to get spanked.

The Worm Turns
by Beverly Langland

Occasionally you find yourself in an odd situation. One you never imagined. You slip into it by degrees in the most natural way. Yet caught in the midst of such bizarre events you are suddenly astonished and wonder how in the world it all came about. So it was that I came to have Julia Pemberton – former school bully and my teenage nemesis – naked and draped across my knees waiting for me to spank her. Up until that point I had failed utterly to humiliate her – even though I had her strip naked for my amusement. Make no bones about it, Julia's humiliation had been my goal from the moment I let her into my flat. It was my sole intention and I was determined to succeed! Even though the sight, the feel of her flawless nakedness, so warm and soft against my thighs, made me tremble.

It seems unlikely that a timid sparrow such as I – the gawky girl denounced to the whole school as a filthy lesbian by the same bully sprawled now at my mercy – would ever have such a chance for revenge. I could hardly believe it myself. I had always consoled myself that violence can never be justified. Yet, given the opportunity for retribution I found myself too weak to resist. As it turned out, the shy, confused teenager I once was *did* discover she was a lesbian. It seems that Julia had known even before me. Though to my mind that didn't mitigate the years of misery Julia put me through.

Imagine my surprise when I met her in a gay club. Admittedly the club's clientele are not exclusively gay and for some reason – probably because they have no rendezvous of their own – some members of the fetish scene have taken to frequenting the 'Velvet' at the weekend. So I didn't jump to any conclusions as Julia approached the bar. I recognised her immediately and such was my awe of her I had to fight an irrational urge to flee. She sat on the stool next to mine and smiled. Such a beautiful smile. Such a beautiful face. It still haunts my dreams. I knew that despite my trepidation Julia's smile would keep me rooted to the spot. Julia offered to buy me a drink and I accepted. After a few moments of small talk she suddenly stopped and looked directly into my eyes. Hers looked as menacing as they always had and I felt my legs turn to jelly. Even if I wanted to I doubted I had the strength to leave. "You don't remember me, do you?" she asked.

I debated whether I should give Julia the satisfaction of admitting I did. I even contemplated slapping her face and making a run for it, or – goddess forgive me – grabbing her immaculate blonde tresses and ruining her beautiful face by smashing it into the bar. I did none of these things. What I really wanted was the same thing I had always wanted – Julia. Besides, I didn't want to admit how much she had hurt me. "No, should I?"

"I suppose not. We were at school together. I'm afraid I was rather horrid to you." She held out her open hand in a gesture of friendship and I instinctively took it in mine. It felt soft and warm, not hard and cold as I imagined it should. She was made of flesh and blood after all. "Julia Watson – Pemberton as was."

"Yes, I remember now. I'm the filthy lesbian." She quickly turned away. I studied the back of her head with some satisfaction imagining her whole face aglow with embarrassment. Maybe she did have a conscience. Julia took a slow sip of her drink, composing herself, before turning back to face me. "Listen, I'm sorry about the whole bullying thing. Truth is, I admired you, admired the way you faced what you are head on."

"Oh, and what's that?"

"A filthy lesbian."

Before I had time to protest I was facing that beaming smile again. I wanted to be angry – not only for that remark but for all the cruel things she had said in the past. Yet somehow I found myself smiling back. "Well, you had a strange way of showing it."

"You frightened me. I was going through a similar turmoil. I felt scared and alone. I didn't want to be different."

"No one does at that age."

"I guess not. I certainly didn't want to be forced into confronting my demons, which was what you made me do when you came on to me. I overreacted, lashed out at you, perhaps the one person I could have confided in. Once the bullying started it was easier to keep the focus on you."

"And away from you!"

Julia took another sip of her drink. "I'd like to make it up to you."

"How do you propose to do that?"

At that moment we were interrupted by a lesbian couple dressed in what I can only describe as bondage gear. They squeezed between us to reach the bar. The younger of the two – a pretty thing – wore a collar bearing the unimaginative inscription 'pussy'. Julia eyed the girl appreciatively, though for her part the girl avoided eye contact. I didn't know whether to feel sorry for the girl or empathise. She looked so vulnerable. So delectable. I tried to attract her attention but she remained with her eyes downcast until her companion led her away.

"Oh, I don't know ..." Julia watched the retreating couple. "Maybe you could make me your slave for the evening?"

I stared at her open-mouthed. "I don't think so!" I find a lot of people have misconceptions about my lifestyle. Despite my sexual preference I am actually a conservative sort of girl. I've never sought anything 'kinky' and to be honest the direction of Julia's conversation made me uncomfortable.

"Why not? I'll let you do whatever you want. I'll even let you spank me."

"No thanks."

"Really? Surely you'd like to punish me. I bet you've been dreaming of it for years."

"I don't need revenge," I lied.

Her eyes twinkled wickedly. "OK. Spank me for fun then?"

"I'm not into spanking." I hoped fervently Julia would change the subject.

"Well, *I'm* wet just thinking about it."

Now, believe this or not, I hadn't gone to the bar looking for sex. Companionship maybe, but not sex. I'm not promiscuous. Yet the thought of Julia wet and aroused was enough to turn the head of a saint. I couldn't help but wonder ...

Julia was beautiful, more so than I remembered, and the pang of adolescent love that I felt for the girl – love that I once foolishly declared to her in confidence – had again risen to the surface. Judging from the heat burning between my legs it seemed the desire she once invoked in me was also still there. Despite the intervening years, Julia still held that unfathomable power over me. I am ashamed to admit that I was still a little frightened of her. It is irrational, I know. I am a grown woman, a successful solicitor – confident both within my profession and with my sexuality. Still, Julia's sudden reappearance after all that time unsettled me.

Needless to say, we went home together later that evening. Julia is the mistress of manipulation and to be honest she made me feel flattered that she found me desirable.

"Your place would be more convenient," she said. Reluctantly I agreed. It was during the short walk there that I formulated my plan. Julia had indicated she was into spanking games. Surely I would have no better opportunity to exact some revenge, to at least vent my pent-up feelings. I needed to strike while I had the chance. So, with some trepidation, I let the bully into the safety of my sanctuary.

I made us both a drink then waited while we made ourselves comfortable, taking the chance to build up enough courage to confront her. I put on some music. "Dance for me," I said after a while.

"Dance?"

"You did say you'd do anything." I attempted to sound commanding, donning a borrowed persona I considered fitting for the occasion. At first Julia seemed confused, yet she played along as if accepting some unwritten challenge, as if she knew it was my intention to break her. I watched her dance, finding her movement highly erotic. I delayed putting the rest of my plan into action for as long as I dared, but then my mind made up, I ordered her to strip.

She smiled, flashing me her perfect pearly white teeth. "As you wish," she said, stepping out of her short skirt with a grace that had me immediately enthralled. She pulled her halter over her head, revealing her beautiful breasts. I was transfixed. It wasn't that they seemed big for her slight body or that they looked as firm and full as they had when I'd first seen them in the school showers. It was that her nipples had grown hard as soon as they were free of the material. Julia was excited.

141

Julia stared intently into my eyes while she slid her panties off. She stood naked, other than her earrings and stilettos, and posed defiantly, hands on hips. I couldn't help myself. I took in the splendour before me. I studied her breasts, stared at the fine hair between her legs, at the enticing ridge poking through. I had waited a long time to see this object of my desire. That's how I wanted her to feel – as an object. My object. Yet, despite Julia's nakedness it was *I* who felt intimidated. She turned slowly, letting me look, and then stood, legs slightly parted, saying nothing. Waiting.

I let her wait. Why not? I was terribly turned on by having my own beautiful doll to play with. Though, when I looked up to her face, her eyes sparkled, just as they had when she taunted me at school. She cocked an eyebrow, seemingly waiting impatiently for me to be done with my useless charade, then approached and draped herself across my lap unbidden. Her breasts hung against my thigh. "Well?" she chided, wriggling her perfect bottom seductively, inviting me to punish her. When did I say I would spank her? I hadn't. After all these years Julia was still calling the shots, still taunting me.

What was I thinking? I tried to regain control. She had me aroused, but that wasn't what this was about. This was discipline. Punishment. Humiliation. Revenge. Not play. Not sex. But I couldn't bring myself to hurt her. I just wanted to gain her attention, to make her realise how her callousness had affected me all those years ago. Julia seemed delighted with my hesitation, as if she had anticipated my every move. Julia always managed to remain one step ahead, always got the better of me. Still, her assumption that I was too weak to follow through incensed me.

I hit her hard with the flat of my hand. Then did it again. Then again on each cheek. Julia didn't put her hands up to protect herself as I had expected, didn't cry out. Instead, she spread her legs a little and pushed herself into my lap. This was not what I'd intended at all. My ineffectualness angered me more. I struck her again. Harder this time. In fact, I lost count of the number of times I smacked her. Certainly until her bottom cheeks were a rosy red, until my hand stung from the effort. During this time Julia made no complaint at all. I admit I gained some satisfaction when she occasionally whimpered, yet she truly seemed to be getting off on the pain. It was obvious Julia was getting wet, so I kept going, driven by my sudden power to make her leak. Finally, she put her hand across her bottom and shouted, "Stop!"

I did. In the sudden quiet I realised I was shaking. We were both shaking. Her buttocks were a flaming red and I noticed that in my frenzy I'd caught her thighs and, with her legs spread, in between them. There were red finger marks dangerously close to the wet opening of her vagina. I felt suddenly ashamed with my loss of self-control, felt at odds with Julia's reaction to the spanking. I could smell her scent. Nice girls didn't react that way. Then, I had never considered Julia as particularly nice.

Still, I was excited by her response. I was grateful that Julia couldn't see my face as I traced the raised outline of the inflamed skin with a fingertip. She said nothing about this. Julia lay passively and just let me fondle her. I was suddenly at a loss and chided myself for not planning ahead, planning past the revenge of the spanking. I had no idea what I was supposed to do now. My intention hadn't been to arouse her. Quite the opposite. Yet it had. Worse – and to my horror – the spanking had aroused me. As Julia squirmed on my lap I too had grown excited. I just had to touch her – for my sake, not hers. So I drew my hand lightly over her moist pussy, surprised how wet she had become. I let a finger trawl slowly between her distended lips, drawing her creamy moisture over the hard bud of her clitoris, lingering, feeling her throb insistently beneath my quivering fingertip. "Please ..." she whimpered as I drew my hand away somewhat reluctantly.

I let out a gentle laugh at the irony. Since she was my first crush I had often fantasised of Julia as my lover, of delving between those long slender legs to explore her hidden depths. If only I'd known back then that getting into her knickers would be this easy, that she would respond this way, it would have saved me much teenage angst. I lifted the wet finger to my lips and held it there, drawing in her aroma. Generally it is the smell of a woman rather than her appearance that excites me. Julia smelt good and even before I slipped the finger into my mouth I knew she would taste good. I wasn't disappointed.

Still, I couldn't believe that I'd actually enjoyed spanking this woman. I never thought I could physically hurt anyone. Somehow this felt different. I felt wicked. Julia had been right. I had spent many hours daydreaming of revenge but even given the opportunity I doubted I could go through with it. Somehow I managed. As thrilling as my power over her felt, it had been Julia's passive compliance that had served to increase my excitement. Julia wanted me to punish her and despite my initial reservations I needed to vent my anger for all those hours of anguish she caused. Yet ultimately, it was the thrill of knowing that what I was doing was taboo that drove me on. Each time I struck her – each time she moaned – drove me deeper into my adopted persona.

While I was still contemplating this bizarre turn of events, Julia slid off my lap and kneeled in front of me. I felt suddenly deprived, almost bereft. She looked so pathetic huddled between my thighs that I wondered why I was ever afraid of this woman. Yet I had been and she, knowing how I felt, had shown me no mercy. Why should I show her any now? Besides, her vulnerability made her look so sexy that I wanted her more than ever. Like the girl at the bar. My mind raced with all the things I would make her do ...

But before I had a chance to capitalise on my victory, Julia surprised me. She stood and walked slowly to the dresser and leaned forward against it, resting. She looked as exhausted as I felt. "Now it's your turn," she said eventually.

"My turn?"

I felt a little frightened by the surge of emotion coursing through me, by the way it centred on my sex. The feeling was intense. Perhaps too intense. For a moment I was in denial. What did she mean? Julia was nodding slowly – smiling. I knew exactly what she wanted. The whole situation felt wrong. When had Julia vested control? In an instant she had turned my victory into defeat and I suddenly found myself trapped in a situation I hadn't contemplated, let alone prepared for. I tried to remind Julia that despite what had just happened I honestly wasn't into spanking. It was meant to be a one-off. Julia agreed. She made it clear that it was the last time I'd ever spank her. She picked up my hairbrush. On the other hand ...

Julia edged towards me, patting the hairbrush against her palm, the sound threatening, sickening.

"Look, I'm not ..."

"Get used to it," she said, waving the hairbrush. "This is what you want, isn't it, why you invited me home with you? Don't tell me you prefer the submissive Julia?"

"Yes. No. I ..."

My mother always told me that people never really change. When it came down to it I was still the submissive devotee and Julia still a terrible bully. Even during the years of abuse I suffered at her hands, or perhaps because of it – because at least that way she noticed me – I still adored her.

"Over my knee! Now! Quickly!" The authority in Julia's voice made me tremble. Real menace lurked behind her words. By comparison my playacting had sounded pathetic, as did my subsequent pleas for mercy. Julia would have none of my whimpering. I was to be spanked whether I wanted to be or not. Almost in a trance I lay across Julia's lap, allowed her to lift my skirt, to pull down my panties. Not for the first time in my life I wished I had never set eyes on her. Julia pressed her left hand into the small of my back, holding me firmly in position. I realised then Julia Pemberton – bully – love of my life – would show me no mercy.

She didn't!

Sleeping Beauty
by Heather Davidson

Please kind sir, don't ask me what's wrong,
For I've sat amongst the trees here far too long,
And in that time I've shed a hundred tears,
One for each of the passing years.

Once upon a time, many years ago, in a land far, far away, there was an enchanted forest. And in that forest, there lived an elf. Yet he was sad of countenance, for a great trouble lay on his shoulders and he took to spending many a day sitting glumly amongst the trees. Then, one fine April morn, he espied a Knight and his faithful Squire riding through the forest, and he asked them who they were.

"I," announced the Knight grandly, "am Sir Roderick de Nance, Prince of Cornubia."

"A Prince!" the elf cried gleefully, leaping to his feet. "A Prince! At last, after all these years, a Prince! Let us give thanks to God for the moment of our deliverance is near!"

"Deliverance?" queried Sir Roderick.

"You must come with me, good Sir Knight," replied the elf earnestly. "For there is a matter to which you must attend."

And so Sir Roderick, being filled with much curiosity, dismounted from his fine white palfrey and followed the elf through the thicket and bramble until at last they came upon the overgrown ruins of an old stone building. And inside this building, fast asleep on a bed, lay a girl of the most remarkable beauty, with skin as white as snow and hair as dark as coal. Sir Roderick ran a gloved hand along the headboard and then carefully inspected his fingers. "Look at the muck in here," he said.

"This is Sleeping Beauty," the elf explained. "And she has lain here for a hundred years; the victim of a cursed spell."

"What happened?" asked Sir Roderick.

"She received a prick," said the elf.

"I know the feeling," nodded the Knight.

"It was only a little prick," continued the elf uneasily.

"Size isn't everything," said Sir Roderick hurriedly.

"Anyway, you must kiss the girl and wake her from her slumber," said the elf.

"Kiss her?" cried Sir Roderick, aghast. "Kiss her? This I simply cannot do."

"But you must," retorted the elf desperately. "Then you will make her your wife and everyone will live happily ever after."

"I don't think so," said Sir Roderick haughtily.

"Why not?" shrieked the elf.

"He can't," interjected the Squire. "He's a bit."

"A bit what?"

"A bit … funny," replied the Squire. "He doesn't like girls."

"Don't care for them at all," agreed Sir Roderick.

"But you cannot leave Sleeping Beauty here!" implored the elf. "She needs a good, strong man."

"Don't we all," sighed Sir Roderick wistfully. "Anyway, we'd best be on our way. Come along Squire, we have things to do."

And with that, the Knight and his faithful Squire departed the scene. The elf gave chase for a little while until he realised the futility of his gesture, at which point he sank to his knees and burst into tears.

Presently, another horse came trotting along the forest path.

"Why so sad small elf person?" enquired the female rider.

So the elf recounted the sad story of Sleeping Beauty and of how Sir Roderick de Nance had failed to break the evil spell. On hearing this sorry tale, the woman dismounted from her mighty steed, and the elf was greatly taken aback, for the stranger was dressed in a short black tunic which barely covered her buttocks and long, thigh-length leather boots.

"Show me this girl," she commanded. "For perhaps I can be of help."

And so the elf led the lady in black through the dense undergrowth until they came to the place where Sleeping Beauty lay. The woman slowly circled the bed, tapping her riding crop thoughtfully against the palm of her hand. Finally, she leant over Sleeping Beauty and kissed the girl hard on the lips. Then she stood back.

Sleeping Beauty stirred and opened her eyes. She focused them first on the elf and then on the lady in black.

"Oh," she said, slightly miffed. "You're a woman."

"Your powers of observation do you credit," replied the lady.

"But shouldn't you be a handsome prince?" asked Sleeping Beauty, sitting up.

"There appears to be a shortage of them," said the elf sadly.

"I am Lady Della de Domme," smiled the woman. "I have released you from the spell and now claim you as my own. You will accompany me to my Castle at Chateau de Domme, where you will live as my companion for the rest of your days."

"Well, I suppose it beats lying around here all day," remarked Sleeping Beauty, rising to her feet.

Lady Della slipped an arm round the girl's waist and guided her back through the undergrowth to the waiting horse.

"Goodbye then, Mister Elf," said Sleeping Beauty as she mounted the mighty steed. "And thanks for everything."

"Do not despair!" cried the elf. "I will not abandon you to the clutches of this evil woman. I will get help and then come and rescue you!"

By the time he had finished speaking, the horse was already out of sight.

They rode for many miles; through wood and forest, pasture and meadow, and thence into the mountains until, at last, they came unto the black castle of Chateau de Domme, perched high on a rocky outcrop.

"Does anyone else live here?" enquired Sleeping Beauty.

"No, just me," answered Lady Della, "and my dwarf servant."

As if on cue, the huge panelled door of the chateau creaked slowly open to reveal a small hideous figure.

"Ah, Mistress, you have returned," purred the Dwarf. "And with a prrrretty girl in tow."

"See to the horse will you, Tallboys," ordered Lady Della. She placed an affectionate hand on Sleeping Beauty's bottom. "Come, my darling, let me show you round your new home."

The guided tour of the castle took several minutes and concluded upstairs in the bedroom.

"Is this my bedroom or your bedroom?" asked Sleeping Beauty, regarding the lone double bed in the centre of the room.

"This is *our* bedroom," replied Lady Della, removing

her long black gloves and placing them carefully on top of a chest of drawers along with her riding crop.

"Oh dear," Sleeping Beauty said worriedly. "I haven't brought any night clothes with me."

"That is not a problem," answered Lady Della, "For I wish you to sleep in the nude."

"Oh, that's alright then," said Sleeping Beauty matter-of-factly.

"I'm sure you must be tired after the journey," smiled Lady Della, conveniently overlooking the fact that the girl had been asleep for the past one hundred years. "Why do you not undress ready for bed?"

Sleeping Beauty hesitated for a moment but then did as she was bid; first she removed her beautiful gown and then she slipped off her pretty knickers.

"But first," said Lady Della, picking up a chair and placing it at the foot of the bed, "It is time for your evening spank."

Sleeping Beauty appeared crestfallen. "Are you displeased with me, Mistress?" she asked, genuinely surprised.

Lady Della let her eyes feast on the gorgeous naked body standing shamelessly in front of her.

"No, not at all," she answered softly. "Quite the opposite in fact." Her voice took on a distinctly harder edge. "Now, come and kneel on this chair."

Once the girl was in position, Lady Della began to spank hard: eight ruthless slaps to Sleeping Beauty's right buttock cheek, followed by a further eight to the left. Then she repeated the exercise – only this time with even more ferocity than before. Then she stopped and let her hand gently caress the girl's reddening rear.

"I call this my sixty-four-er," she explained. "Eight crisp spanks to the buttocks, eight times."

"Forgive me, Mistress," whimpered Sleeping Beauty,

"but I fear that I have received only half that number."

"I haven't finished yet," replied Lady Della coldly. "But as you are clearly impatient for the rest, then we will resume."

She slapped Sleeping Beauty hard on the bare bottom. "And that wasn't one of them!"

The spanking began again; four batches of eight hard smacks, all expertly delivered by a woman who, over the years, had become well qualified in the art of discipline.

"So beautiful," whispered Lady Della, using both her hands to knead Sleeping Beauty's shapely rear. "So warm and so beautiful. Oh, how I've longed for this day; to finally have a girl in my castle who will submit to my special brand of discipline."

Lady Della crossed over to her chest of drawers and picked up the black riding crop from where she had left it. "And now I want to introduce you to something that you're going to get to know very well during your time at Chateau de Domme." She waved the riding crop under the girl's nose. "This!"

Lady Della brought the riding crop down hard against the girl's well-rounded buttocks.

"How does that feel?" she asked.

"Oh, Mistress, it hurts," replied Sleeping Beauty truthfully. "But …"

"But what?"

"But … in a nice sort of way."

"Hmm," murmured Lady Della. "Very interesting."

She placed a hand on Sleeping Beauty's scarlet backside and felt the girl shudder with pleasure. Lady Della raised the riding crop. "Then let's see how nice you think this is!"

The woman began to thrash mercilessly. Howls of anguish echoed round the castle, and it was only when they turned to cries of pleasure that Lady Della lessened the pace. From then on, each new stroke of the riding crop produced a shriek of ecstasy, until one final, brutal blow brought Sleeping Beauty to a shuddering climax.

Lady Della stood back and waited for the girl to regain her composure.

"If this is what happens when you are pleased with me," remarked Sleeping Beauty dryly, "then I should hate to know what happens when you are … displeased."

Lady Della laughed and kissed the girl softly on the lips.

"You'll find out soon enough," she said. "But now I wish to consummate our relationship."

"Consummate?" frowned Sleeping Beauty. "I'm not quite sure I know what you … oooh!"

And so Sleeping Beauty settled into her new life at Chateau de Domme. Most of the time she walked round in just a top with her bare bottom on display, and other times completely naked. And if she displeased her Mistress then she was spanked, and if she pleased her Mistress then also she was spanked, but not as hard. And afterwards, Lady Della would make love to her, sometimes tenderly, sometimes roughly, depending on how the mood took her.

Then, one fine spring morn, a visitor arrived at the entrance to the Chateau. Sleeping Beauty, being for once correctly attired, opened the door.

"It is I!" cried the elf excitedly. "After a year and a day, I have found you." He held up a small glass phial containing a colourless liquid. "Tonight, when Lady Della takes her evening meal, you will slip this potion into her wine. She will immediately fall into a deep sleep; not, alas, for as long as a hundred years, but long enough for you to escape!"

"Sod off," said Sleeping Beauty and slammed the door shut in his face.

"Well, that's gratitude for you, isn't it?" complained the elf to no one in particular. "Anyone would think she didn't want to be rescued."

"Who was that?" enquired Lady Della, descending the stairs.

"Just some elf," replied Sleeping Beauty. "I got rid of him."

"Do you know what today is?" asked Lady Della, taking Sleeping Beauty in her arms and kissing her passionately on the lips. "It is exactly a year and a day since I found you in the forest and brought you to my castle."

"I am aware of this," answered Sleeping Beauty quietly. "And, in all that time, I never realised how happy I could be."

"Then let us mark this occasion," Lady Della suggested, "with three hundred and sixty-six spanks to your bare bottom – one for each day of your new life."

"Ooh, Mistress!" shrieked Sleeping Beauty.

And everyone lived happily ever after. Apart from the elf, of course.

Mistress Satina's Slutmaid Academy 2:
A Caning for the Goddess
by Alexia Falkendown

Mistress Satina's Diary.

Strict discipline is my secret for success in running my select Slutmaid Academy. A strong hand is essential – be it to chastise aspiring Slutmaids' bared bottoms or stroke their throbbing sissycocks. Behind the discreet satin drapes of my residence in Brighton's Royal Pavilion Square, I whip and massage my postulants into shape, so that when they receive their Slutmaid Diploma they have that feminine poise and charm which sets elegant ladies apart from baser, grosser, undepilated males.

Aspiring Trannies spend a fortune on satins and silks, wigs and facials, stockings and heels, but without my training and make-over how-tos, accompanied by regular application of cane and dildo to their bared bottoms, they cannot achieve that feminine silhouette, beauty and poise that distinguishes my Academy graduates from a Widow Twankey in the Theatre Royal Christmas Panto or a hirsute transvestite looking uncomfortable in a misfit dress bought at the Oxfam shop.

It is not only my novitiates who require regular visits from Mistress Smack to their submissive slutbutts, but also my Tranny staff. Serena and Candy left mundane jobs *en drab* in the City to work *en femme* for me. They are a good support team for Adelaide, my collared bride and Academy

Supervisor. But they are sometimes naughty Trannymaids and I need to slap a warming blush to their pretty posteriors with my leather tawse before caning their bouncy bottoms. I fear that they are now so addicted to the painful pleasures of my erotic flagellation technique that they have become gluttons for punishment!

I needed to discipline them last December during our annual Yuletide weekend house party for Academy alumni. We had squeezed ten Slutmaid graduates into our three guestrooms, (a bit of a squeeze, but what girl doesn't squirm with pleasure when accommodating a tight fit). On the Saturday morning, Adelaide disappeared with two of our alumni for a fitting appointment at Axfords, Brighton's famed bespoke corsetieres whose stylish Edwardian lace-ups turn even the dumpiest of Slutmaids into a sexy wasp-waisted, curvaceously bottomed siren. Adelaide had arranged for Serena to prepare the buffet luncheon while Candy ran a make-over workshop for the others. Unfortunately, neither remembered to collect the six dozen fresh oysters ordered from Sid's Stall at the Open Market. I was very angry. I called Adelaide and my two Trannymaids to my office after lunch.

"Your disgraceful mismanagement has ruined my reputation as a hostess. I shall punish you for your waywardness. This is a grave misdemeanour. You will endure the acute emotional discomfort of anticipating the sting of my cane before you are summoned to the Temple tomorrow evening to suffer the humiliation of having your bared bottoms whipped before our assembled Slutmaid alumni."

I adhere to an imaginatively stylized spanking ritual at both the Slutmaid Academy and in my private household.

"It is Dark Moon tomorrow night and you will offer your bodies to the scourge of Nemesis, at our monthly Dark Moon ritual in the dungeon Temple. Candy, you will be my acolyte for the evening. I have caned you often enough in the Temple for you to know the routine. Put the heaters on, ensure that the wall sconces have fresh red candles, drape the marble altar with the black and gold altar cloth and purify the Temple with incense. Punishment ritual will start at 9 o'clock. All Slutmaid alumni must attend. I expect them to be properly made-up, wearing heels, black seamed stockings and their short-skirted black satin uniforms with frilly bouffant red lace petticoats that show their stocking tops and a hint of red slutknickers. That will be all! Return to your duties!"

A spanking ritual is the essential core of all Domina/Submissive relationships. It is through the flogger, tawse and cane that a total bonding is forged between a Dom and her Sub. They respond to such heightened moments of sensual drama, feeling the deep impact of their close presence upon each other.

Such a ritual can be formal, like my monthly Dark Moon Temple ceremony, or informal and intimately personal. In our private boudoir and bedroom sessions, Adelaide's thrill comes not only from her willing and trusting submission to my safe and loving control, but also from the intoxicating power emanating from me that enters her receptively compliant body through the hypnotically thudding strokes of my flogger, the sharper focus of my tawse, or the thrilling pain of my cane. I am her mirror. She is the chalice for my energy which I channel into her with each stroke. We become one as her soft body responds to the flogger's caress, tawse's kiss and rattan's sting. She tingles in breathless expectation and acceptance of the painful pleasure imparted by my lovecane's endorphin-releasing sting to her heated cheeks and the cooling caress of my satin-gloved hand to her striped bottom and those moist pussylips so provocatively exposed between her parted legs. Through the portal of our shared ritual, we

157

enter together into a realm of pure power that takes us to an erotic plateau of unforgettable and indescribable orgasmic intensity.

We honour Nemesis each month at Dark Moon with a flagellation ritual in our 'Dungeon' Temple. As Nemesis is the ancient Goddess of the Scourge and Retribution, this is a uniquely auspicious occasion to mete out punishments for grave misdemeanours brought to my attention during the preceding month. I was pleased that on this particular occasion we had guest participation. They would have the good fortune to share our physical and spiritual ecstasies reached through the threshold of pain-pleasure as my collar bride Adelaide and Trannymaid Serena offered their bodies to the scourge of the Goddess in expiation for their misdeeds.

Adelaide's Diary

Mistress was in a festive mood at the prospect of whipping us on the altar before the Goddess statue in the Dungeon. Before Mistress bought the house and blocked up the basement entrance, 'The Dungeon' had been an eponymous private drinking club for gays when sex between consenting males was still a crime. Now reached by the back stairs, its entrance is guarded by a statue of Anubis, the ancient jackal-headed God of the Underworld. There are three vaulted rooms in what were originally 18th century wine cellars. Mistress turned one room into our 'Dungeon' Temple for her Dark Moon and Underworld rituals, and converted the other two into 'Dungeon' playrooms where she does all sorts of complicated and painful things to her fetishslut clientele, from whom she exacts a suitably expensive 'tribute' for her esoteric services.

As a Priestess of Nemesis, Mistress's sensual pleasure is always heightened by the presence of an audience appreciative of her flagellatory prowess. Their participation would add a frisson of sexual excitement to our caning, charging the room with pent-up lust for our naked bodies squirming erotically before their salacious gaze as we writhed helplessly beneath the stinging scourge of Mistress's cane.

Mistress has often told me that she finds my rounded cheeks and pussylips, framed by lace suspender belt, seamed stockings and high heels, a most sensually arousing picture. I must admit that when I watch Mistress cane Candy or Serena, I am equally aroused by the alluring sight of their bouncy butts blushing red beneath her measured strokes. I like to think that Mistress finds me more desirable than the others, however, when I present my plump posterior for the whipping I know she so much enjoys giving and I enjoy receiving. My pain becomes our mutual pleasure and her caning sets us on fire with desire for each other.

Mistress's 'Afterglow' boudoir parties for her household are as much a part of her spanking ritual as her caning. Having surrendered our bodies to her flagellatory pleasures, we retire to her candlelit boudoir where we surrender our bodies anew to her imperious clitoral demands and mutual orgasmic ecstasies. I'm in heaven when she queens me and I suck her pink pearl to climax after climax while Serena and Candy suck her boobs, my clit and their pussycocks.

Serena and I were dressed and prepared for punishment when we entered Mistress's dressing room at 8 o'clock to help her, as usual, at her pre-ritual *toilette*. The difference this time was that *we* and not *they* were to be caned.

I had twisted my long auburn tresses into a tight chignon to better display the hammered gold torque that was the symbol of my collaring when Mistress took me as her submissive bride last year in an intimate Temple ceremony. I had provocatively '*un*dressed' for Mistress's visual pleasure. I wore a black lace platform bra to emphasise the ripe fullness of my exposed breasts with the large brown aureoles and nibbly nipples that Mistress, (and the others) so love to suck and tweak. My matching suspender belt framed the smooth softness of my shaved Venus lips that Mistress, (and the others), so love to tongue. It was cut high at the rear to show off my now fashionably plump J. Lo *derrière* that Mistress so likes to spank, (and the others to fuck); my bare booty was provocatively framed for the occasion by the retro straps holding lace-topped black seamed stockings taut against my ample thighs. High-heeled can-can boots completed my ensemble.

Serena had her shiny black hair plaited into a pigtail and had dressed in red. Her budding powder-puff breasts and pointed nipples were slung in a cupless bra and her sheer red stockings were held up by a red lace suspender belt that accentuated the roundness of her sweet arse and framed her very sociable pussycock. Nine months of packing oestrogen pills had rounded and filled out her once lanky sailor-boy physique, giving her a trendy curvy bottom that Mistress had taken a shine to.

Disrobing Mistress of her black pencil skirt, rose-pink silk blouse, designer bra and camiknickers, we laced her into the black sateen Basque corset she wears for flagellatory exercise, fastening its six suspenders to her black stockings. Her corset fits like a cobra's skin, moulding itself to the sleek contours of her well-kept body; emphasizing her trim waist, the swell of her rounded hips and the curve of her firm buttocks, so well tuned for thrusting dildo action on Tranny butts. It erotically displays her 'Brazilian' that leads down to the 'camel toe' of her ever-hungry lovelips from which her hooded pearl protrudes so invitingly beneath her see-through knickers.

The custom-made corset's open cup underwiring supports her bared breasts, giving them proud prominence while leaving them free to swing as she whips her chosen victim.

Having tightly laced Mistress into her basque, I ran my hands down over the swell of her bottom and then lightly over the full voluptuous roundness of her breasts. Her thrusting nipples stiffened at my fleeting touch. She cupped a breast, inviting my lips to its heavy succulence. "Suck me, my Sweet!"

I smiled happily at her endearment and began to suck greedily; my hand dipping into her tight knickers to caress her cunt, now moistly hungry for my mouth to assuage the hidden tension that was building in the core of her uterus.

"Kneel behind me," she commanded Serena. "Pull down my knickers and clasp my bottom in your undeserving hands and spread my cheeks wide to expose my hidden glory hole and lick it! Suck its tightness!"

Serena hastened to obey. She knelt and, pulling down Mistress's knickers, parted her toned cheeks to expose the hidden puckered orchid of her magnificent arse, so erotically framed by corset and taut stocking suspenders. She nuzzled her head between the spheres and began her oscular devotions.

"Genuflect and tongue me, my Sweet! Worship at my altar while Serena buzzes around the fragrance of my flower," she commanded me.

She pressed me down to the wetness of her now exposed cunt and stood, legs apart, hands on the swell of her corseted hips; an awesome, silver-haired Domina exacting tribute from her vassals.

I have a serpentine tongue! It was time to show it! Mistress's blood-engorged clitoris peeked out invitingly from its pink hood; a '*bijou petit pénis*' seeking my lips. An orgasm now would put her in a more benign mood when she took up her cane to punish us.

"Sweet Mistress!" I murmured, rubbing the tip of my nose up against her clitoris. I began to lick, nibble and suck at that most precious of pearls, coaxing it from its pink hideaway into prominent arousal before darting my tongue into the musky recesses of her bower to luxuriate in her fragrant wetness.

"Sweet Mistress," I whispered again in adoration. "I worship at your altar."

Mistress gripped our heads, forcing us to nuzzle ever deeper into her furrowed recesses. She closed her eyes, a smile of pleasure radiating over her aristocratic features as our ministrations fanned the glow in her belly to a flame.

"Suck me, my darlings," she panted hoarsely. "Bring me to orgasm!"

Our combined oscular frenzy brought Mistress finally to her explosive climax. She stiffened and pressed my face fiercely against her pubic bone, rubbing my nose at her throbbing clit. She clenched and unclenched her buttocks against Serena's darting tongue, urging her 'cherry-licker' ever deeper. Her juices began to trickle, flow and then flood.

"Drink! My beloved," she whispered huskily, her eyes closed in ecstasy. "Drink your fill from my sacred chalice!" She shuddered as the orgasmic wave crashed over her, washing through the deep rivers of her body. She came with a throaty sigh, flooding me with a hot cumsquirt that left me gasping as I lovingly lapped at her streaming joyjuices.

Mistress stood, tautly motionless; an erotic statue on her high orgasmic plateau.

She slowly relaxed and opened her eyes.

"Enough! You are well-trained sluts! You have worshipped well. The fire you lit has smouldered, flared, flamed and died. Your altar lustrations are over until after I have caned you."

The antique French Empire mantel clock on the ormolu cabinet whirred. Three chimes heralded the quarter; 8.45pm.

Mistress raised us from our knees with a sated smile. She kissed Serena and then me, savouring the flavour and fragrance of her own lovejuices on my lips.

"You are diverting me from my duties! I shall whip you both even harder for such deviousness!" She always says this after we have given her a pre-punishment cunnysuck and orchidbuzz, but her post-coital kiss belies her threat.

"You'll be late for your appointment! Be ready when I sound the Temple gong. Tonight's ritual is unchanged except that you must expect a severe caning instead of mere erotic titillation."

She kissed us again. "But think of the 'Afterglow' pleasures we shall later share in my boudoir. While I whip your pretty butts, remember our Academy's motto: 'Spare the Rod and Spoil the Pleasure'! Your pleasure will come later from my loving hands and lips and Candy's ever-obliging pussycock!"

Cunnilingus is one of the most beautiful and satisfying experiences we women can share together and, as Mistress's collared bride and Household Supervisor, I ensure she is kept well satisfied in this respect, particularly before a punishment parade when it's *my* bottom in Mistress's sights.

Mistress is always hyper-tensed before a punishment ritual and has little time then for 'special effects'. But when we are relaxed in her boudoir, I cunnysuck her for an hour or more at a time, breaking off to kiss her breasts and lips while Serena and Candy explore below. Later when we are alone together in our four-poster bed we suck each other, sharing multiple orgasms, enjoying the fullness of our mutual arousal, orgasm and flow. Thus do our bodies become one in a blissful union of Mistress and Bride.

A gong sounded. It was 9 o'clock. The Temples double doors were opened and we could see into its womb-like red stuccoed interior. It was dimly but warmly illuminated by the flickering candlelight of wall sconces. Two ceiling spotlights cast a red glow over the black and gold altar upon which we would act out Mistress's sacred punishment ritual.

Candy was at the door to lead us to the altar. She wore the Temple acolyte's robe of black velvet. It clung sensuously to her Tranny breasts, belly and bottom, now so curvaceously and desirably feminine after her hormone treatments. An interesting bulge where her pussy should be, showed the outline of her sweet trannycock and balls. We would milk them later.

"When I purify and consecrate your bodies with incense, breathe deeply of its fragrance," Candy whispered conspiratorially. "Its narcotic and euphoric ingredients will calm you and take you to a dream level where pain becomes pleasure and time stands still.

The moment had come. Serena was quivering from the dread thrill of fearful anticipation. I clasped her hand and we stepped forward to our fate.

Mistress Satina's Diary

I was standing at the Nemesis altar, cane in hand, when Candy led the two miscreants silently up the aisle. When they reached me, Candy genuflected before me and moved to the charcoal burning sensor standing on a side table. She placed an 'egg'of Kyphi resin on the hot coals and swung the sensor, igniting the sweet smelling incense of Ancient Egypt.

"Do you freely offer your bodies to the sacred scourge of Nemesis on this Night of the Dark Moon?" I asked.

"We do, Priestess!"

"Then humbly place yourselves over Her altar and

prepare to honour Her with your cries of pain."

The girls bent over and settled themselves, taking the weight of their bodies on their straightened arms so that their breasts hung free in pendulously erotic abandon.

Acolyte Candy stepped forward. "Spread your legs to part your bottom cheeks. You must expose your sacred orifices to the gaze of the Goddess to be properly presented to Her. Raise your heads and arch your back to display your bottom for the cane."

The girls obeyed quickly and 'presented'. I could see the pink tightness of Adelaide's puckered flower above the swollen labia that would later welcome an 'Afterglow' tongue, pussycock and dildo. Adelaide's lovelips, visible beneath her bottom's under-curve, were lewdly open, a driblet of juice glistening in the spotlight's glow. Serena's heavy balls and long pussycock dangled enticingly free between her stockinged legs. I wondered whether my caning would bring her usually lively member to excited erection on this occasion!

Candy swung the smoking sensor at the Goddess statue, over the altar and then over the bared buttocks displayed before us. "We consecrate this caning offered upon Your altar. May Your Sacred Scourge bring the cleansing pain that leads to divine ecstasy."

The girls held their pose, inhaling deeply the thick smoke of the incense's sweet narcotic fragrance wafting over them. A tremor of fear coursed down Serena's stockinged thigh, her butt muscles twitching.

"Present your bottoms!" Candy called loudly.

The two girls arched their backs once more, raising their shiny bottoms.

I took my caning stance to ensure that the girls would receive each stroke's full impact on both cheeks. I rubbed the cane along the flagellator's 'Sweet Spot', that exceedingly tender line where bottom curves into thigh, and I visualised smacking the soft flesh there.

"I shall cane you alternately, stroke by stroke and pause between each set of strokes for you to assimilate the pain received and anticipate the pain to come. Adelaide, you will count each stroke aloud for you both and thank the Goddess for Her cleansing scourge. Is that understood?"

"Yes, Priestess!"

There was an eerie silence as my 'sacrificial lambs' and I awaited Candy's command. I drew back my cane.

"Commence Punishment!"

Crack! Crack!

I brought the cane across in two quick strokes to stripe each exposed bottom, doubling the whippy end's stinging impact with a flick of my wrist.

The rattan whipped across their soft cheeks in a searing streak of fire that hit unerringly on the 'Sweet Spot' in a jolting explosion of pain. Both shot bolt upright, clutching their burning globes, eyes closed, mouth open in silent agony. For a moment, they made no sound. Then they screamed …a piercing cry of pain. They rubbed their bottoms feverishly at the angry scarlet stripe that appeared across their cheeks as if by magic. I had now left a burning red line as my marker.

"Resume your position immediately or I shall add strokes for being uncooperative!"

"One! Thank you, Goddess!" Adelaide murmured as they draped themselves once more over the altar.

I stepped forward to run my hand over the angry weals I had just raised on the two bottoms, feeling their heat before stepping back and taking aim again.

Crack! Crack!

A second scarlet line seared its fiery path across their buttcheeks, just above the first. The miscreants grunted but steadfastly maintained their position, despite the pain I was inflicting.

"Two! Thank you, Goddess!"

Crack! Crack!

I delivered the third stroke with a wrist flick that etched a painful crimson welt above the second. Adelaide shrieked at the burning agony I had inflicted upon her gorgeously plump booty. Three parallel red lines now scorched the dimples of her now involuntarily twitching cheeks.

"Three! Thank you, Goddess!"

Crack! Crack!

I whipped across another stroke, eliciting a further anguished scream from them. They were now panting, beads of perspiration dampening their faces as the shock of pain coursed through their bodies.

"Four! Thank you, Goddess!" Adelaide sobbed.

Crack! Crack!

It was the hardest stroke yet. Serena screeched and started to rise, intending perhaps to shield her tortured rump from the rattan's scorpion-like sting, but thought better of it.

"O-oooh" Adelaide cried, as a fifth angry welt joined the others across her curvaceous bottom, now quivering in spasms of pain. I paused to caress her ravaged cheeks, luxuriating in the feel of heated stripes and her helpless squirming; movements I found most sensually arousing.

"Five! Thank You, Goddess!"

I glanced at my acolyte. She stood mesmerised. While not erotic for the victims it was certainly arousing her, judging from the growing bulge of her pussycock pinioned inside her knickers beneath her robe.

I positioned myself for the final stroke, cutting diagonally across the five parallel welts; the infamous 'Gate' cut.

Crack! Crack!

Scarlet lines of pain on each butt joined up a pattern of livid agony; a fiery crimson memento that would turn to deeper shades of purple by morning.

"Six! Thank You, Goddess!" Adelaide broke into a deluge of tears, thankful that her ordeal was over.

I admired the colourful picture I had etched and stepped forward once more to caress the heat of the raised welts, running my palm lovingly over the results. I surveyed with pride the sharp parallel lines of pain crossed by the final diagonal cut I had scored across the tortured plumpness of Adelaide's rump and the daintier spheres of Serena's Tranny arse.

Candy stirred herself and swung the sensor again to sanctify the girls' tortured flesh with Kyphi incense .

"Rise now and kiss the Scourge of Nemesis!"

The girls rose painfully, turned and knelt to kiss the scourge. I laid it on the altar, where it would lie until next required.

I took Adelaide and Serena into my arms, holding them close, kissing their tears away. Caning those bottoms had made me wet with desire. My throbbing cunt ached now for the orgasmic release that I always need after the power surge of such a 'Domina High'. No caning is complete without that release, for both caner and caned. It was high time for 'Afterglow' party play! I never waste good playtime! I led my hot threesome out of the Temple and up the Stairway to Heaven!

'Afterglow'? That's another story! But I *will* tell you that Adelaide milked two pussycocks to their desired release while I gave her the thrusting pleasure of my strap-on dildo! Then we *really* got down and dirty!

168

The Psychiatrist
by Heather Davidson

I sat nervously in the waiting room, occasionally flicking through the various lifestyle magazines on offer or simply watching the pretty receptionist as she dealt with the constant stream of people and telephone calls. I glanced at my watch. It was now ten minutes past my scheduled appointment time. Dr Black must be running late. I was suddenly reminded of my paternal grandmother. When faced with a similar situation, she would always go up to the reception desk and ask, rather pointedly, whether the doctor had "forgotten" her. I laughed out loud. Several heads all turned to look at me. They probably thought I was mad. My GP obviously thought I was. Just lately, I'd had difficulty sleeping. I'd become forgetful, unable to concentrate on things. My GP had listened sympathetically and then suggested that I see a psychiatrist. "It's nothing to worry about," he'd said. "Just someone to talk to. Someone who might be able to find out what it is that's bothering you."

I was suddenly brought back to reality by the voice of the receptionist. "Mrs Davidson? Consulting Room Five."

Dr Black was exactly how I'd imagined him; tall, distinguished and in his mid to late fifties. With his half-rimmed spectacles, he looked every inch the psychiatrist or even, I thought, an old-fashioned schoolmaster. He had my GP's letter of referral on his desk and we began by chatting about my recent problems. Then he suggested that I might like to "pop myself" onto his couch.

"I bet you say that to all the girls!" I quipped.

Dr Black peered at me over the top of his half-rimmed spectacles. "Please try and take the session seriously, Mrs Davidson," he said sternly.

Shut up, Heather, I thought. Just shut up.

So I went and got on the couch and the good doctor came and sat beside me with his notepad and pen.

"We'll start with a simple word association test," he said briskly. "I'll say a word and I want you to tell me the first thing that comes into your head. Right?"

"Left," I answered automatically.

"I haven't started yet, Mrs Davidson," he sighed.

"Sorry," I mumbled.

"Now, here we go," said Dr Black. "Eggs."

"Er, Bacon," I answered.

He sniffed and made a note on his pad.

"Carpet?"

"Slipper."

"Monarch?"

"Ruler."

"Leather?"

"Tawse."

"Garden?"

"Cane."

"School?"

"Discipline."

Dr Black paused for a moment and rubbed his chin. "Come and sit back down at my desk," he said, rising from his chair.

"I now know what is wrong with you, Mrs Davidson," he continued a few moments later.

"You do?" I asked doubtfully, sitting down opposite him.

"You have a spanking fetish," he replied. "Every answer you gave me was in some way related to corporal punishment. You are completely obsessed with the subject."

I buried my head in my hands. This was most embarrassing.

"I'm going to refer you to one of my colleagues who specialises in this sort of thing," said Dr Black, pulling open a drawer and extracting a small business card which he handed to me. "Dr Lambert. You can make an appointment with the receptionist on the way out. Good day, Mrs Davidson."

So exactly one week later, I found myself sitting in the same waiting room, staring at the same people and wondering how you could be cured of a spanking fetish. One of the consulting room doors opened and an attractive brunette, probably in her early thirties, poked her head out.

"Mrs Davidson?" she called.

I rose to my feet.

"Please come through."

She shut the door behind me and grasped me warmly by the hand. "Caroline Lambert," she smiled. "I'm so pleased to meet you." She gestured towards the empty chair on the other side of her desk. "Please sit down."

Once I was seated, Dr Lambert looked down at a folder on her desk. "Now, I've been reading your case notes and I think I can help you," she said. "Although the treatment might be a little … unorthodox."

"Unorthodox?" I prompted.

Dr Lambert leant back in her chair and put her hands behind her head. "The conventional approach would be regression therapy. You know, take you back to your childhood. See if there's some past event that triggered your fet– … problem. But you're basically a spankophile and I intend to treat you the opposite way to how I would treat someone with a phobia."

"Sorry?" I asked.

"Let's say that you had a phobia about … snakes for instance. I would take you to the reptile house at the local zoo. Show you lots of snakes. Let you hold one, caress one, fall in love with one."

Somehow I couldn't quite see myself falling in love with a snake. And why the hell had she picked snakes? Everyone knows what they symbolise. Perhaps she needed to see a psychiatrist.

"I intend to prescribe a course of severe corporal punishment," continued Dr Lambert. "By the end of it you will have come to hate spanking in all its forms. Words such as slipper, tawse and cane will become associated with terrible pain, and thus you will be cured."

"That is a novel approach," I agreed, somewhat uncertainly. "So I'll, er, make an appointment to come back next week then, shall I?"

"Good gracious, no!" exclaimed Dr Lambert cheerfully. "I intend to start your treatment immediately."

"Immediately?" I shrieked in reply. I needed time to think this through properly. Get things sorted in my head. But Dr Lambert was having none of it.

"Stand up please," she ordered. I rose to my feet with some apprehension. "Now turn around."

What was this, I thought. A blooming fashion show?

"That's a nice dress," commented Dr Lambert admiringly. "But I'm afraid it'll have to come off. Remove it, please."

I hesitated for a moment, conscious of the fact that I was wearing no bra, before slipping off my cotton summer dress and draping it over a convenient chair. Dr Lambert cast an approving eye over my near naked body. It was then I realised that she might be a lesbian and the thought excited me.

I soon found myself bent over the good doctor's desk receiving a brisk hand spanking on my shapely rear. My skimpy knickers afforded little protection and most of the slaps landed on bare flesh.

"That's reddening up quite nicely," remarked Dr Lambert, running a hand over my backside. "But I think we'd better have these down."

Immediately, my hand went to my knickers in an ill-judged attempt to try to prevent such a humiliation but a hard slap to the buttocks soon made me see the error of my ways. The good doctor pulled down my knickers and made me step out of them, which was easier said than done when the skimpy little things became entangled in my high heels. Finally they were tossed aside, and I was back over Caroline Lambert's desk but now completely naked. She began to spank me hard on my bare bottom. It was an interesting technique: two fiery strikes to the right cheek followed by three quick slaps to the left. Then the ritual was repeated, only this time in reverse. It was painful, but in quite a pleasant way.

"You like that, don't you?" observed Caroline.

"Mmm, yes," I replied, until suddenly remembering why I was here. "Well, maybe not."

"Hmm," said Dr Lambert, walking round to the other side of her desk, opening a drawer and extracting a long black leather paddle. "Then I think it may be time to move on to the next stage."

I glanced nervously over my shoulder as she walked back round behind me.

It's a good job that this was on the National Health Service, I thought to myself. Imagine having to pay for such treatment!

I yelped as the leather paddle landed squarely across my bare buttocks.

"Just what the doctor ordered," laughed Caroline, rather pleased at her own joke. She stopped laughing and started to thrash me with the paddle. I shrieked and squealed as the wretched implement found its target over and over again.

"Don't worry, you'll soon be cured!" cried the good doctor cheerfully.

From my position, I had an excellent view of the floor on the other side of Dr Lambert's desk and rather fancied that the carpet needed a good clean. Caroline's bag was placed neatly behind her desk but it had been left open and I could see a magazine stuffed just inside. A rude magazine! At least, I assumed it was rude; not many other journals would have a beautiful bare-bottomed girl adorning the front cover. My earlier assumption about Caroline Lambert was obviously correct; she was indeed a lesbian, or at least an aficionado of women's bottoms. And who could blame her? Even I felt an intense attraction to the sexy cover girl and her magnificent rear.

As these thoughts ran through my head, I began to realise that the paddle wasn't hurting any more. Quite the opposite, in fact; I was actually looking forward to each stroke! The girl on the magazine cover smiled back seductively and I felt my nipples harden with desire. A wonderful feeling spread across my buttocks and threatened to engulf my entire body. The strokes were harder now but ever more delightful, and the final one brought me to a shuddering climax.

"Did you just have an orgasm?" demanded Dr Lambert angrily.

"Yes," I blurted out.

Caroline Lambert tossed the paddle away in disgust. "Then I'm sorry, Mrs Davidson, but there's nothing I can do for you," she said. "You're a hopeless case!"

Hard Times at the Nymphomaniac
Rehabilitation Facility
by K. D. Grace

It could have passed as a coach excursion through the scenic Surrey Hills, but Sadie knew better. This was her bus to an indefinite period of miserable celibacy, at least that was what she thought when she and three other women stepped off the coach in front of the main wing at the Nymphomaniac Rehabilitation Facility.

They were met by a tall woman dressed in a riding habit and a conservative tweed jacket that failed miserably to disguise her delicious curves. Her dark hair was pulled back in a severe bun. Her boots were polished to a high sheen, and she carried a riding crop under one arm that made Sadie's heart skip a beat. She certainly hoped the woman knew how to use it.

"Listen up," the woman shouted in a voice that was standard military issue. "I'm Ms Greuber, assistant warden." Her face became earnest, like she was doing an advert for some local charity. "You may not know it, but nymphomania is nearing epidemic proportions in Surrey, and here at the Nymphomaniac Rehabilitation Facility, the problem is being dealt with discreetly, and thoroughly. You're all here because you've admitted you can't control your sexual appetites, and we're here to help you curb those appetites and channel your energy in more productive endeavours." She paced in front of the four women, stopping to inspect each one in turn.

Sadie was already horny from the bouncy ride on the coach, and the big, beautiful woman standing in front of her so assertive, so tough, did nothing to ease her pussy or her distended nipples, doing their best to drill through her thin summer shirt.

"You're not wearing a bra."

Sadie shook her head. "It's too hot."

Ms Greuber gave Sadie's 38Cs a rough squeeze. "Nevertheless, in future you'll wear a bra, or you'll suffer the consequences." She gave Sadie's tits a smart flick with the riding crop that made them sting and bounce dangerously beneath her shirt. Her pussy got wetter. The woman then cupped Sadie's breasts as though she were weighing them. "You'll need proper coverage and support."

Ms Greuber turned and paced onward. "All residents will attend evening prayer. You'll find it makes the nights easier. The dorm is in the South Wing. Your uniforms and new undergarments are on the foot of your beds. You will be unpacked, changed and in the chapel in one hour."

Trussed up in a knee-length pleated skirt of some scratchy synthetic fabric, a heavy cotton blouse and a bra and knickers her grandmother would have found prudish, Sadie trudged off to the chapel, seriously thinking of running away, and she hadn't even been here two hours.

The chapel was hot and stuffy and full of sweaty female bodies dressed just like she was. She found a seat in the back and sat despondently while the organ blared something that wasn't Bach. They had just stood for the processional when a dark-haired woman, breathing heavily, slipped into the pew next to her. She grabbed a hymnal, opened it and moved close to Sadie, holding it up for her. "You're new," she breathed. Sadie barely heard her over the voices, but there was no denying the feel of her warm

176

breath against her ear, nor the way the woman brushed her small, pert breast against Sadie's arm when she leaned in to whisper, "I'm Carol." Her lips brushed Sadie's earlobe.

"I'm Sadie."

"Shortage of hymnals in the back rows," Carol said, holding the book open for Sadie to share.

"I don't sing," Sadie replied.

Carol moved in closer. "Neither do I." She turned slightly, insinuating her breast against Sadie's arm once more.

"You're not wearing a bra. I got in trouble for that."

"No knickers either," Carol whispered. "Want a feel?"

Her proposition made Sadie forget all about broken rules. She pressed closer to Carol, pretending to be immersed in the words of the song. Slowly, carefully, she inched her fingers up Carol's skirt until she felt her bare silken thigh and saw her eyelids flutter and her breath catch. She was suddenly very thankful for the long shapeless skirts. They made exploring easier, and the magnificent thigh was a promise of things to come. She felt Carol shift slightly, and she knew instinctively she was opening her legs just enough for Sadie to have a good feel.

Sadie's old-lady knickers were drenched clear through their practical cotton crotch as she slipped her fingers onto Carol's smoothly shaven mound, even softer than her thigh. The woman shuddered at her touch. Sadie could smell the salty sweetness of aroused pussy, pussy other than her own, and her mouth watered for a taste. She was just about to slip her fingers into Carol's waiting pout when the song ended and everyone sat down. The two breathlessly followed suit.

Chaplain Carlton approached the lectern. As he droned on about purity, Sadie had a hard time paying attention, with Carol's hand stroking her thigh.

"His cock's nice and thick," Carol whispered very

softly, nodding to the chaplain.

"You've fucked him?"

"God no, but I've seen his cock plenty of times. He may be celibate, but he's always ready for a good wank, especially when it comes to overseeing the penance of naughty girls." She slipped her hand under Sadie's skirt.

"He's not bad looking," Sadie whispered. The man was deep-chested, greying at the temples and wore Indiana Jones glasses, which suited him well.

"He loves to watch when we're being punished. Watch and wank. That's a part of what makes this place so much fun."

"Fun?"

"You'll see." She took Sadie's hand and pulled her off the pew onto the kneelers as they all began to pray.

Carol laid her head on the pew in front of her as though she were deeply repentant, but it wasn't prayer she was interested in. With sleight of hand that would have impressed any magician, Carol's fingers were once again under Sadie's skirt and straight into her knickers.

But just when Sadie was about to get some relief, Ms Greuber appeared out of nowhere standing at the end of the pew, looking positively explosive.

"I'm in trouble," Carol whispered, giving Sadie's clit a little tweak. "Trust me, around here, the punishment is worth the crime." She gave a discreet nod toward the assistant warden and licked her top lip hungrily. Then Carol was jerked from the kneeler and practically dragged down the aisle of the chapel as everyone stood to sing the closing hymn.

That gave Sadie the opportunity to slip out quietly and follow Ms Greuber and Carol at a safe distance. She was way too intrigued not to risk it.

She followed them across the car park and down to the paddock, just managing to duck behind a hedge as the two women turned into the stables. Sadie had forgotten that the brochure for the place had promised that riding in the fresh Surrey air was therapeutic. As she peeked around the door, she saw Ms Greuber and Carol in the tack room. She ducked into an empty stall, behind a bale of straw, to watch.

"As part of your punishment, Carol, you'll be keeping my tack clean and well polished for the next week." The woman ran her hand lovingly over a saddle mounted on the rail of a stable, in which stood a large black stallion shifting from foot to foot. "Vindicator and I go for a ride every morning and evening." She held Carol's gaze. "And I'll know if you haven't done a good job." She slapped the crop against her hand.

"As for the rest of your punishment …" she slipped the end of the riding crop under the edge of Carol's skirt, lifting it until even Sadie, in her hiding place, could see Carol's lovely bare cunt. "Wearing no knickers is just one of the many rules you've broken tonight, Carol Owens."

Carol stood trembling, with her pussy exposed, as Ms Greuber undid the top several buttons of her blouse and ran a hand inside. Then she nodded as though she were a doctor pronouncing a diagnosis. "No bra either, and that in front of a poor girl I just reprimanded for not wearing a bra. What must the poor thing have thought? How you must have tempted her. I know how much you love to fondle full, heavy breasts like hers, but you must learn self-control." Ms Greuber made no attempt to remove her hand from Carol's tits. Sadie could see that she had manoeuvred the edge of the riding crop between Carol's pussy lips, and Carol was practically humping it.

"Stop that," Ms Greuber commanded. "Bend over and grab the stable rail."

Carol did as she was told, and Ms Greuber shed her jacket and turtleneck, beneath which she wore a silky vest

179

which revealed a deep, delicious cleavage even more dramatic than Sadie's. That done, she lifted Carol's skirt up over her hips until her round little bottom was exposed in its entirety, then she tapped the riding crop against the inside of Carol's knees making her spread her feet apart until her swollen pout was perfectly displayed. Then the riding crop came down with an angry thwack and Carol whimpered.

"You played with that poor girl's pussy, didn't you? Didn't you?" The crop came down again.

"I couldn't help it. She was so hot."

"Did you let her touch you down here?"

Carol nodded.

"Did she make you come?"

Sadie's hand had already found its way into her old-lady knickers, but her cunt positively gushed when Ms Greuber inserted her middle finger up into Carol's pussy and probed.

"I was so close, but then you saw us." Carol moaned, rotating her hips against the finger, her little nether hole clenching as she did so.

There was a soft shuffling, and Sadie turned to see Chaplain Carlton standing in the shadow of the stable door, fly unzipped, heavy cock straining in his hand. Bloody hell, the punishment was worth the crime, Sadie thought as she tweaked her clit, which felt almost as hard as the good chaplain's penis.

"You wouldn't lie to me, would you?" Now Sadie's attention was divided between the wanking chaplain and Carol's punishment as Ms Greuber inserted another finger. "You feel awfully wet for someone who didn't come." She brought down the riding crop again on Carol's bottom, now pink with welts. Carol whimpered and squirmed, and the chaplain tugged harder on his cock.

"I swear I didn't come," Carol whined.

But Sadie could tell from the way she clenched and rocked against Ms Greuber's fingers that Carol's orgasm was close.

Ms Greuber pulled her up from the railing to face her. "We can't be responsible for tempting others. We all have to conform to the rules." She grabbed Carol's hand and pressed it against her expansive breasts, huge nipples now assaulting the silken vest. "You see, I wear a bra, and knickers." She guided Carol's other hand into her trousers, a place Carol was clearly happy to explore, and the catch of Ms Greuber's breath, the flutter of her eyelids, told Sadie Carol had found what she was looking for.

"Make me come," Carol whispered. "Please, make me come and I'll make you come too. I swear I'll clean your tack for the rest of my stay, with my tongue if you want, just please."

The assistant warden's hand was instantly under Carol's skirt, stroking furiously, and for a second the two women strained against each other, gasping and moaning, then Carol let out a little yelp. "Oh God, Ms Greuber. I'm coming. It's so good." The woman only responded in heavy grunts as she trembled against Carol, the mounds of her tits nearly tumbling over the top of her vest.

Just then the chaplain erupted like a fountain in viscous spurts against the stable door. That was enough to send Sadie's pussy into spasms.

When the chaplain tucked in his cock and slinked away, and Ms Greuber left mounted on Vindicator, Sadie sneaked out from her hiding place to where Carol stood happily polishing an extra saddle. She didn't seem surprised to see Sadie.

"Greuber and the chaplain, they can get you off, but if you want cock," she gave Sadie's tits a caress, "then you need to see the warden."

"And how do I do that?"

"Trust me, I have a foolproof plan."

Their plan had gone like clockwork. Sadie kept her eyes lowered, but not out of respect for the warden. She was looking at his cock straining the seams of his trousers. Carol said he always got a hard-on when it came to doling out punishment.

His crisp pinstriped suit accentuated his broad shoulders. He was clean shaven, every blond hair in place, and he smelled as though he'd just stepped out of the shower. Sadie so admired dapper men.

She, on the other hand, with her mussed auburn hair coming loose from its demure ponytail, with the pleats of her modest skirt hanging uneven, with her white blouse, untucked, gaping dangerously above her full breasts, looked guilty as charged. She was trembling, but not from fear – well, just a little, maybe.

The warden paced. "The chaplain says you were masturbating in the library."

She whimpered. "Please, sir, I couldn't help it." She quivered at the memory. The chaplain had thought she couldn't see him half hidden behind the shelf, his hand thrust deep in his pocket, moving in tight little jerking motions as he observed her. Knowing he was watching her play with herself had only made her stroking more pleasurable.

Carol had been right, once the chaplain had come, he grabbed her by the shoulder and marched her straight in to see the warden.

"The poor man was horrified." The warden stopped pacing, grabbed her by the shoulder and pulled her closer. "Where's your brassiere?" He gave her left tit a hard squeeze nearly causing it to pop out of the gaping blouse as he ran his thumb over her nipple, pinkly visible through the fabric. "Do you realise how provocative this is? You'll incite other residents to lewd acts."

"My bra's so uncomfortable," she whined. "It doesn't fit right. When I wear it, my nipples ache. I rub them to make them feel better, and I get so turned on. My titties are so sensitive. Please, it's not my fault."

"I'm sorry, but you have to be taught restraint." He moved a step closer, slipped his hand up under Sadie's skirt and stroked the wet crotch of her knickers.

She let out a breathy little moan as he traced an accusing finger along her slit.

"You're still slippery from your transgressions," he grunted. "The chaplain said your pussy was all wet and splayed and swollen for the world to see." His fingers pressed deeper into her, knickers and all. His breathing accelerated. "He said you were leaning up against the shelves in the reference section with your panties pulled aside, your fingers way up inside you, thrusting and moaning so hard you didn't even see him." He lifted her hand to his nose and sniffed, then groaned as he gave her a hard stroke. "I can still smell your shameful efforts," he said breathlessly.

She couldn't help it. She shifted her hips against his hand and opened her legs for the full benefit of the warden's probings. "I'm so sorry. It's just that I needed to come so badly, and if Chaplain Carlton had only given me a minute more, I could have had some relief."

The warden shook his head. "What shall I do with you, Sadie? You're such a little slut. You'll have to be punished. I have no choice. We can't expect reform when someone is running around this facility with her nipples showing, and her fingers up her fanny." He suddenly remembered to take his hand away from Sadie's pussy, and she whimpered in frustration, squeezing her legs together and shifting from foot to foot while she clenched and relaxed the muscles of her quinny, desperate for relief.

He grabbed her hand and dragged her to a wardrobe near his desk. "Take off your blouse. Go on, take it off."

She unbuttoned it slowly, pretending to be embarrassed, ashamed; an act that made her tingle all the way up to her tits. She let it slip off her shoulders shyly, cupping her heavy breasts in pretend modesty, making sure her nipples peaked through her fingers for the warden to see.

"Remove your hands."

She did as she was told, clasping her hands demurely in front of her, a stance that deepened her impressive cleavage while she rocked back and forth. She kept her eyes lowered to the warden's ever-expanding cock, now clearly visible beneath his trousers. The sight made her pussy even more slippery, and she clenched her legs tighter.

"What size?" He demanded, fumbling through a drawer of bras.

"38C. But please, sir, I'm sure the one issued me is too small. It holds my titties so tight that I can barely breathe. Please can you size me for a bigger one?" She took his hands and guided them onto her breasts with a soft little moan.

"In future, keep your breasts covered properly." His big, rough hands cupped her tits and kneaded them, thumbs and forefingers lingering to tweak and pinch her nipples until he seemed to have trouble breathing. "We simply must find something modest. Your nipples are so … so very erect, so difficult to hide." Reluctantly, he pulled away and fumbled through the drawer until he produced a bra of pink diaphanous lace. He stroked each of her breasts in turn and settled them into the sheer cups, reaching behind her to hook the band. As he did so, she could almost feel the heat of his distended cock through his trousers. Then he stepped back. "Oh dear. That's not much better, I'm afraid."

If anything, her nipples pressed harder at his scrutinising stare. The tops of her breasts mounded like ripe fruit above the lace of the cups. "Perhaps that will get you by until Ms Greuber can fit you for something more modest."

"Now for your punishment." He sat down on a leather sofa near his desk and patted his knees. "You know the rules. Touching oneself is a punishable offence. You must learn your lesson or you'll never be fit for civilised society. Come now. Over my knee."

Whimpering softly, keeping her eyes lowered modestly to the warden's penis, she bent over his lap. Her pussy twitched as her pubis pressed against his muscular thigh. Through his trousers, his cock squirmed against her stomach. The feel of it made her ache all over with want. He settled her into position with a grunt of satisfaction and grasped her wrists securely behind her back with one large hand. She quivered with anticipation as he hiked her skirt and eased her panties down until she felt the cool air against her bare bottom.

He cupped each of her buttocks in turn and gave them a squeeze, his thumb lingering to exert intriguing pressure against her nether hole. "Such a naughty girl." The words barely left his mouth before his hand came down with a resounding thwack against her bare arse, and she cried out at the sting of it, shifting her hips and bearing down to press herself harder against his thigh, feeling the growing thrum of arousal as she did so.

"It hurts, I know, but naughty, slutty girls must be spanked." She could feel the shifting of his own hips, pressing his cock harder and harder against her belly. She wriggled and whimpered with the next thwack and felt her pussy gush against his thigh. The thought of her pussy juices wetting the pinstripes of his trousers nearly sent her over the edge. Her clit felt stone hard and hugely distended from beneath its hood, as she relished the press of him against her.

The stinging of her arse was exquisite. As she squirmed, one hand came loose from his grip. She manoeuvred it beneath her stomach to rest against his cock, and his next thwack was accompanied by a groan. This one came from him. Encouraged, she gave his heavy erection a stroke as he smacked her bottom again, and the fingers of his other hand slipped between her slick quinny lips, just exactly where she needed them.

She was now practically humping his leg with each smack of his hand. She could imagine how lovely her bright red arse cheeks must look to him, blushing up so tender and wounded. Each time he spanked her, he splayed them just enough to stimulate her arsehole and make her clench. Sadie could feel him thrusting too with each thwack, until at last neither of them could disguise their moans of pleasure. "Please make me come," she whimpered. "I need it so badly. I won't have to touch my pussy if you make me come. Please. I know I'm such a bad girl, but I can't concentrate on being good when my pussy is so hot."

"Get up, you little slut," he gasped. He dragged her to her feet. For a second, he stood panting before her. Then he shoved aside the delicate bra straps and forced her breasts upward to spill from the cups, taking them in turn, into his suckling lips, making every effort to get as much of each titty as he could into his mouth. With one last suck and a nibble he shoved her forward and bent her over his desk, her stinging tender arse in the air. She heard his trousers fall, heard the sound of a condom being donned.

"You're such a naughty girl, such a little whore." She felt his hot breath on the back of her neck, just before he slammed his cock deep into her swollen pussy and began to thrust.

Then he splayed her arse cheeks, still hot and stinging from her punishment. She heard him wetly sucking his finger. That done, he slipped the wet appendage into her grudging pucker hole with such delicious pressure that she orgasmed hard and bucked back against him.

"Did you come, you little slut?" He spat against her pucker and shoved another finger into her, still pumping hard in her cunt. Up inside her arse, she could feel his fingers moving, stretching her tightness, arousing her deep in her hole.

"I'm not done with you yet," he gasped. He pulled his cock from her slit, drenched and slippery with cunny juice and shoved it deep into her arsehole. She cried out in a cocktail of pleasure and pain. The fullness of the first thrust was agonisingly delicious followed by pleasure nearly unbearable.

As she reached between her legs to fondle her dilated cunt, he slapped her hand away. "We don't play with ourselves at the Rehabilitation Facility. Remember? That's what you're being punished for in the first place," he grunted.

He could now barely breathe, and his thrustings felt like they would split her in two, as the next orgasm broke over her in waves that nearly propelled both of them off the desk onto the floor. Just then, he groaned and she felt his cock convulse inside her as he shot his load, then collapsed on top of her gasping for breath.

When at last he could breathe again, he dressed and helped her to her feet, wiping her wet pussy carefully with his neatly ironed handkerchief. "I do hope this has taught you a lesson, Sadie. Get dressed and go clean yourself, then the chaplain wants to talk to you about your penance."

Sadie couldn't wait. Contritely tucked into her new bra, her bottom still stinging from the warden's heavy hand, she was off to see the chaplain, content in knowing that the punishment was, indeed, worth the crime.

Truly Scrumptious
by Mark Ramsden

It is not that socially acceptable, yet, to talk about male domination of submissive females. It still looks a bit nasty to the uninitiated. Because many liberals are still in thrall to the 1970s idea that men are all secretly Jack the Ripper. They seem to think, because of some bad-tempered college girls, that the hand spanking of a willing female leads inexorably to torture and murder. And I've just breathed further life into what should be a rotting corpse by now. Never mind. I was a lettuce-eating liberal myself once, before reality reasserted itself. But I still need a disclaimer before I can tell you about gently warming Truly Scrumptious's tight little bottom cheeks with the palm of my right hand. While slowly insinuating the fingers of my left hand into her moistening cleft until … but that would rob the moment of why it was so interesting in the first place. If we don't know who Truly Scrumptious is, none of the other stuff would matter particularly. And it's not the same if you're not just a *little* bit in love, now is it?

Her real name is Holly but I wanted to give her a new name: Truly – as in Truly Scrumptious. My son had recently forced me to watch *Chitty Chitty Bang Bang* far more often than was good for me. The name of the attractive nanny seemed to fit her very well – as she was and is gorgeous – although I didn't learn the 'true' significance of 'Truly' until later. Her habit of telling the truth, always, no exceptions, was refreshing but sometimes made you long for the traditional system of saying whatever caused the least grief.

I lost my heart to Truly on our second meeting. I was already smitten the first time I saw her, when she walked on stage during a slave auction at a fetish club. She had short black hair cut any old how. Her smile was wide and salacious, full lipped with a cute little gap in her front teeth. Some of the others were arranged in the traditionally haphazard British manner. I found this honest and endearing, like her charity shop clothes. I might have a shaven head and some serious tattoos but I'm an old hippy at heart – like my wife, Katrin. And like Truly. Although they are younger and considerably easier on the eye.

Even in a nightclub Truly wore almost no make-up and her only accessory was a school prefect's badge on her jacket lapel. The lettering read 'Perfect' instead of 'Prefect'. I couldn't argue with that.

Her blue eyes seemed to be saucers full of nourishing liquid. Or were they shot glasses full of some ferociously strong hooch? I had been off the hard stuff for some time, being married. But you never really get over the craving, you just decide life's smoother without it. Or you keep telling yourself that till you believe it ...

After my wife and I had bought Truly's company for the price of a few pints of foul British beer we had the option of some lewd chastisement – to which she had already assented as part of the auction. But instead we talked about what it felt like to offer yourself to strangers. Even in the safe confines of a fetish club it was still an edgy thing to do.

Then we talked of her recent romantic entanglements. She preferred sex with other women's men. It seemed to me that this bizarre preference was in order to shield her from commitment, although she dressed it up in a lot of nonsense about breaking the shackles of conventional morality and no one being anyone else's property. Fine. But not everyone believes in what used to be called free love. In fact, very few people do. Not only is there no such thing as a free lunch there may not be free love either. Although you probably have to be over a certain age to find that out.

Later that evening I dipped my head between her legs and licked and nuzzled her for what seemed an eternity – time having melted due to some pure MDMA powder, a substance yet to drive me mad with overuse. That would come later ... or was it the loss of Truly Scrumptious that pushed me over the edge? This was long before the blizzards of email, the endless phone calls, the hopes, the wishes, the dreams.

Before we left the club that night we talked of astrology, which was handy as I had knocked out birth charts for a living once upon a time. An auspicious beginning you might say, especially as we met on the day of a full moon. And that particular April had two full moons, a rare occurrence which had to mean something sensational was about to happen. One full moon usually provides an adequate sufficiency of lunacy, as anyone working in a hospital casualty department will tell you. Two full moons were likely to test my already fragile grip on reality.

The very next day Truly Scrumptious turned up at our flat for a reading. She looked different in daylight, but still warm and cuddly and smart and cute and lovely in a manner that was hers alone. There can sometimes be nasty surprises when you meet people who have bewitched you in the flattering light of nightclubs. Especially with the aid of Ecstasy. Luckily she was still beautiful. Her features were still fine enough to stand being foregrounded by the scruffy student haircut. I was already very fond of her by the time she had sat her bejeaned bottom down opposite me.

Over freshly ground coffee we discussed, briefly, bands I had never heard of, politics I had long since abandoned and why consumerism meant the end of the planet. I had lived long enough to prefer central heating to squats with broken windows but I let her talk. I had thought the same at her age, so I couldn't really complain.

She might have disdained consumerism but seemed to like trying out whatever new therapy had just been invented – the more the merrier. Although they didn't seem to fix whatever it was that was wrong with her. She worked for a charity but played very hard indeed – sex, drugs, fags, booze. Truly had a light Northern accent but appeared to have a vaguely genteel background. Just like me. And she was actually scanning her way through our many bookshelves.

"You're a writer!" she said, eyes shining.

"Not any more," I said. But not so retired that I don't want people to read what I have already produced. My books are left where our visitors can see them. No one ever picks them up. But Truly had found one of the novels and was flicking through it avidly.

"What are you writing now?" she said. She actually wanted to know. I was already lost – not yet 'in love' – but afflicted with something or other. Something heart-shaped anyway.

"I packed it in," I said. "But *you* write." She raised her eyebrows.

"How did you know?"

Probably because anyone other than an aspiring writer would have ignored the book. She was looking a little awestruck. I was obviously psychic. It is amazing what you can do with a bald head and a bit of enigmatic silence.

"You keep a journal," I said. It seemed a safe bet.

"Wow!" she said. I had passed the audition. I would be

able to sort out her life. I had already spread her chart out on the table, with eighteen pages of pretty elastic one-size-fits-all speculation attached to it. That was all straight off an expensive computer programme but there were also two or three pages of notes I had made, which had involved consulting many weighty tomes and a pack of tarot cards that your average occult tourist knew nothing about, one I had painted myself.

"Don't tell me if it's anything bad," she said, huddling herself up inside her thrift shop jacket. Sometimes people say this with a smile but she was genuinely afraid of something.

"Well, you have a Scorpio moon, which can be dark and dangerous."

The Scorpio woman is the Dark Goddess we all fear. Whereas the merely human have blood running through their veins, the Scorpionic have fermented moon juice with a slug of tabasco. This peppery, zesty fluid also powers those with a moon or ascendant in Scorpio or any other prominent planetary placing. Of course, many men are afraid of women, Scorpionic or not; I know I am. But there is good reason to fear those with a lot of Scorpio in their charts. Know them by their horns and cloven feet. They may also smoke Marlboro Lights. Thankfully Truly's Scorpio moon was balanced by the caring, cuddly Cancer sun.

"Where's Katrin?" she asked. "I really like her."

"She's whipping an old tart called Ernest," I told her. Although I didn't mention that this was an entirely financial arrangement. Or that Ernest still wore fishnet stockings at the age of 72.

"You have an open marriage?" asked Truly, surmising correctly.

"For fetish play, yes. And we discuss everything. No secrets. Playing is fine. I don't do intercourse. But playing lasts much longer anyway. So it's not so much of a sacrifice, anyway."

A wicked little smile slowly spread as she saw the logic of this.

"She's out?"

"Yes. Till tonight."

"And she won't mind then?"

"No," I said. For this is what Katrin had said that very morning. Although she may not have actually meant it, of course.

"I can be a slut then?" she asked. She was easing into her minx persona. The bad girl who was about to use her body in ways that would have broken her mother's heart. I blame Roman Catholicism myself. Although, as it produces a regular supply of especially wicked women, perhaps we shouldn't complain *too* much.

Her eyes widened. Her lips were moist. After a flirtatious shake of head sideways she gave me the full-moon eyes again. They were big and blue, although the whites were strewn with red wreckage. This was a reminder that she had a plentiful supply of her own demons. Perhaps she didn't always like what we were about to do. But was driven to do it anyway.

She stood up and kicked her red Converse sneakers off. Then eased her jeans and knickers down. She laughed as she threw her T-shirt in a corner and unhooked a bra that was never going to feature in a lingerie catalogue. But with firm, full breasts like hers she did not need to spend money to look stunning.

Naked, she stepped into my space. The warm scent of her breath sent the blood racing around my body. Something bigger than the two of us was setting this in motion. The force that impels sperm to impregnate a fertile womb. Well, not on this occasion, Grandma. Mother Nature was just going to have to wait. But the Devil himself was coming out to play.

"I've been bad," she said, taking her voice back some decades. And jutting her lower lip out.

"You've been wicked, my dear," I told her. "You need firm handling. Someone to take care of you."

I don't always feel comfortable mouthing these shopworn lines. But it was what she needed to hear. Besides, I can credibly personify authority in short, sharp bursts. Particularly when there is a flawlessly pert bottom to be unveiled. With a rapidly moistening slit pouch peeking out from between her long, lean legs.

"Do I need a spanking, sir?" she asked, her eyes twinkling though her voice seemed anxious.

"You certainly do," I said. "It's the only language you understand."

She laid herself over my lap and sighed gently as she made herself comfortable. Some think you should start a spanking with outstretched fingers, gauging the required force of the slaps by the sighs of gratitude or the squeals of pain. I prefer a multi-disciplinary approach myself, a little of everything. A cupped palm here, a little pull and prod there. Tweaking the springy bottom flesh between finger and thumb made us both sigh. With so much moisture coagulating in her pussy cleft it seemed a shame not to put a thumb inside her. Soft sighs of satisfaction mingled with my own less than graceful groaning. We both needed this. Badly. A few more taps with my fingers and it was time to cup my hand. And strike where the curves were at their roundest.

Part of me was thinking it would always be like this: the lover's fallacy that strikes when the blood first drains from the head to more erogenous zones. Perhaps that's why the rational part of the brain ceases to function. We never did get to repeat this peak moment often enough for me, but the memories still remain.

Sometimes, when lost in lust, she would turn around and pull the cheeks of her bottom apart. Do me. Do me now.

I found this sort of thing passed the time quite adequately. It was an absorbing hobby. One I never got tired of. Although Truly was infuriatingly unreliable when it came to arranging our diary. Understandably enough, she was looking for a life partner and not someone to do sex with occasionally. And then there was the new-age tripe. "I am choosing to experience life on a higher plane," she would tell me, when cancelling dates to which she had only just enthusiastically assented. Still, there's nothing like spirituality, is there? 'Choosing to experience life on a higher plane' indeed! Even on the first day she offered herself to me I was irritated by her recommendation of some new-age twaddle called 'Conversations with God', which had, needless to say, sold several million copies. My own 'Conversations with My Lord Lucifer' was unlikely to sell a similar amount, even if I ever got around to writing it. Thinking of this particular idiocy I smacked her squirming bottom three times in quick succession, hard enough to hurt the palm of my hand. I'll give her 'choosing to experience life on a higher plane', I thought, starting to warm to my task. An indignant 'hey' soon disabused me of the notion that this was acceptable behaviour.

Well, sometimes you have to do what is good for the person over your lap rather than what they think is good for them. And the warm glow spreading from her chastised cheeks appeared to be bucking her up no end. But I slowed down anyway, as the customer is always right, once they have placed their trust in you. In any case, just watching her get lost in the moment was exciting enough to make my heart pound.

"Yes! Yes! Yes! Oh, thank you! Thank you!" she said, giving sincere thanks for something for which she had

195

waited too long. I was beginning to feel a little blessed myself. Fortunate to have found her. I stroked her slowly, front and back, until a note of desperation entered her voice.

She flirted and squirmed, finding postures that would encourage me to penetrate her. Or slap that impudent little rump of hers just a little bit harder. I was in no hurry. Although Truly appeared to disagree, urging me on by performing some frankly indecent contortions.

This may be one of the reasons Truly preferred father figures. Most young men would have come by now and be halfway out the door to boast about it in the nearest pub. Whereas, being forty-something, I don't have the energy to scamper anywhere except here, where everything is set up just the way I like it.

While Truly got deeper into her trance I patted the reddened flesh for a while, still hardly able to believe my luck. Then a scratch of a fingernail here and there reminded her that into each life a little rain must fall. And that a little vinegar mixed with oil makes a fine combination. The sour-sweet tang of her scent was heavier now and her posture inelegant to say the least – thrusting her rump up in the air and kneading the bed-sheet with her outstretched fingers. Well, we all have needs and I've often done what she was doing. Tarting around on all fours demanding to be serviced. Fill me up. Fuck me. But it's best not to answer these prayers too quickly. Stroking up and down the divide of her bottom with my left hand while keeping the soft slaps coming with my right seemed to be doing her a lot of good.

The soup was simmering nicely now. I thought boiling would spoil it. Truly seemed to disagree. She straddled my body, face down towards my feet, legs wrapped around my stomach, backing herself up towards my face as I continued to pat her with cupped hands. Harder smacks seem to be finally answering the question she posed some time ago. Her skin was rosy red, the heat spreading where it was needed most. The scent of her twin openings was a mingling of the sacred and the profane; heavenly, yet grounded on earth.

"Go on! Do it!" She was getting impatient. Coming to the boil.

I kissed and licked her as she urged me on. Now the surface of her hot red bottom was moist with saliva the slaps had more effect. A mewl of distress told me to tone it down. Which I was happy to do. It was just as nice stroking and kissing the warm velvet flesh for a while before a different sort of urgent moan and upward thrust of her hips was telling me to pile on the pressure again. As I resumed the gentle but firm pitter-patter of slaps and smacks the sounds she was making were closer to those of a hungry beast. Once she unzipped me I was no longer so aloof, not so much in control as I perhaps should have been. But, as my old Zen master used to say to me, when you are hungry you should eat. And with a hot dish in front of me, and with the chef urging me on, it was time to tuck in.

I buried my face in the cleft in her beautiful bottom while Truly took my hardness in her mouth. The sounds of guzzling and slurping competed with our grunts and groans.

Once her teeth had caught my piercings once too often – which was once, actually – I withdrew and she took me in hand, rubbing me slowly up and down. Meanwhile it seemed appropriate to form the fingers of both hands into wedges to press gently inside each of her openings. Once I had done that her eyes screwed up and her mouth opened to its fullest extent. One thing that was bothering me was my wedding ring slipping off inside Truly's warm, wet pussy.

But it was too late for that now. And it would have been nice if that astral image of a disapproving Katrin could have disappeared but you can't have everything.

Now my right hand was inside her pussy it was easy enough to wiggle my first two fingers down onto the spongy tissue which some chap claimed to be the G-spot – naming it after himself, as if Grafenberg was ever going to be a sound you would want to associate with pleasure zones.

And then there was no more time for talk. The storm enveloped us. We came. Then came to our senses, both starting to feel guilty in different ways.

Should young ladies really behave like that? And what about married men? Who were old enough to know better?

My phone alerted me to a voice message withdrawing permission for what had just happened. Although my wife had been keen enough – or apparently apathetic enough – to agree to it that very morning.

"What's the matter?" asks Truly.

"Katrin," I say. "She's gone off the idea."

I didn't have to explain. Truly was used to the anger of wives and significant others. Was it even part of the thrill for her?

Kicking Mummy out of Daddy's bed?

I breathed in her Body Shop soap and hints of her innermost secrets still on my fingertips as she dressed, looking for ways to remember her. Just before she left she put both hands on her still glowing bottom and pushed her lower lip out. She stood with her feet turned inwards, regressing back to some time she must have felt cared for, secure.

"You're very … thorough," she said.

"Any time," I said, making detailed plans for a number of futures that never happened. At least I still have her cheeky smile. Even though I had thought it was the start of something. The start of everything perhaps. Instead of a few years of near-misses and misunderstandings and trying to ignore primal urges while dealing with tearful goodbyes and endless arguing about relationships. We did have our wild moments together. Now and then. But fewer times than you could count on the fingers of one hand.

She's driving someone else mad now. There isn't a cure in sight, just yet. She rang to say she was pregnant the other day. But she couldn't quite get her head round the concept of marrying the father just because society expected her to.

She had assented to the marriage then decided not to go ahead. After all the arrangements had been made.

When I stopped laughing at that I wondered if her parents sometimes regretted that she was now too old to spank.

Or whether her new bloke took care of her in that way.

Someone should, anyway. That's the truth ...

More great books from Ⓧcite...

Naughty Spanking One
Twenty bottom-tingling stories to make your buttocks
blush!
9781906125837 £7.99

The True Confessions of a London Spank Daddy
Memoir by Peter Jones
9781906373320 £7.99

Girl Fun One
Lesbian anthology edited by Miranda Forbes
9781906373672 £7.99

Sex and Satisfaction Two
Erotic stories edited by Miranda Forbes
9781906373726 July 09 £7.99

Ultimate Curves
Erotic short stories edited by Miranda Forbes
9781906373788 Aug 09   £7.99

Naughty! The Xcite Guide to Sexy Fun
How To book exploring edgy, kinky sex
9781906373863 Oct 09   £9.99

For more information and great offers
please visit
www.xcitebooks.com